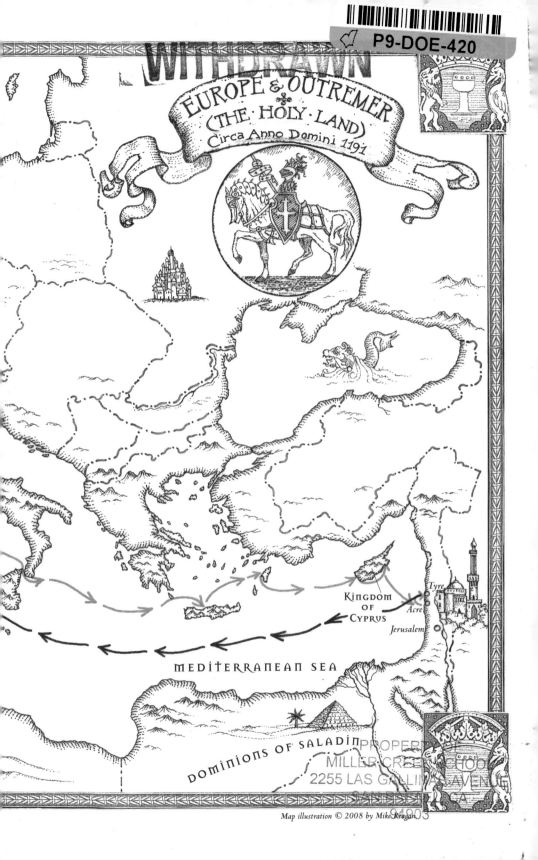

EUROPE & OUTREMER
(THE · HOLY · LAND)
Circa Anno Domini 1191

KINGDOM
OF
CYPRUS

Tyre
Acre
Jerusalem

MEDITERRANEAN SEA

DOMINIONS OF SALADIN

Map illustration © 2008 by Mike Reagan

# DATE DUE

| JAN 3 '71 | | | |
|-----------|---|---|---|
| '77 | | | |
| '78 | | | |
| MAY 10 '72 | | | |
| DEC 16 '75 | | | |
| | | | |
| | | | |
| | | | |
| | | | |
| | | | |
| | | | |
| | | | |
| | | | |
| | | | |
| | | | |
| | | | |
| | | | |
| | | | |

# The
# YOUNGEST
# TEMPLAR

## Book Two
## Trail of Fate

### Michael P. Spradlin

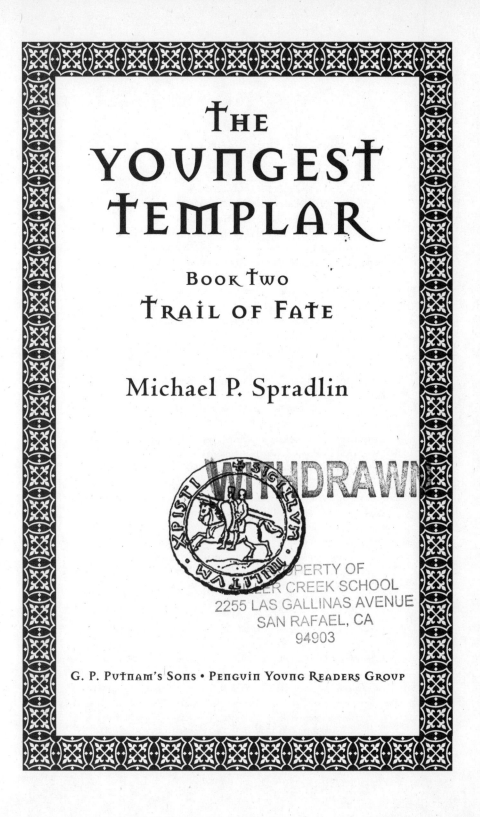

G. P. Putnam's Sons · Penguin Young Readers Group

G. P. PUTNAM'S SONS
A division of Penguin Young Readers Group.
Published by The Penguin Group.
Penguin Group (USA) Inc., 375 Hudson Street, New York, NY 10014, U.S.A.
Penguin Group (Canada), 90 Eglinton Avenue East, Suite 700, Toronto, Ontario M4P 2Y3, Canada
(a division of Pearson Penguin Canada Inc.).
Penguin Books Ltd, 80 Strand, London WC2R 0RL, England.
Penguin Ireland, 25 St. Stephen's Green, Dublin 2, Ireland (a division of Penguin Books Ltd.).
Penguin Group (Australia), 250 Camberwell Road, Camberwell, Victoria 3124, Australia
(a division of Pearson Australia Group Pty Ltd).
Penguin Books India Pvt Ltd, 11 Community Centre, Panchsheel Park, New Delhi—110 017, India.
Penguin Group (NZ), 67 Apollo Drive, Rosedale, North Shore 0632, New Zealand
(a division of Pearson New Zealand Ltd).
Penguin Books (South Africa) (Pty) Ltd, 24 Sturdee Avenue, Rosebank, Johannesburg 2196, South Africa.
Penguin Books Ltd, Registered Offices: 80 Strand, London WC2R 0RL, England.
Published simultaneously in Canada. Printed in the United States of America.
Design by Marikka Tamura. Text set in Centaur MT.
Library of Congress Cataloging-in-Publication Data
Spradlin, Michael P.
Trail of fate / by Michael P. Spradlin ; [map illustration by Mike Reagan].
p. cm. — (The youngest Templar ; bk. 2)
Summary: In the Middle Ages, young squire Tristan of the Knights Templar, King's Archer Robard,
and Muslim assassin Maryam work together to protect the Holy Grail as they travel across France
toward England, a journey that takes them to the Cathar fortress of Montségur.
[I. Knights and knighthood—Fiction. 2. Grail—Fiction. 3. Albigenses—Fiction. 4. Middle Ages—Fiction.
5. France—History—Philip II Augustus, 1180–1223—Fiction.] I. Title.
PZ7.S7645Tr 2009 [Fic]—dc22 2008052888
ISBN 978-0-399-24764-4
1 3 5 7 9 10 8 6 4 2

# Acknowledgments

Once again, I find myself overwhelmed by the support, hard work and dedication so many people have given to this book. It truly is a collaborative effort, and I'm very lucky to have such a tremendous number of resources to draw from.

Thanks to my agent, Steven Chudney, for always keeping me on track. Thanks to my editor Timothy Travaglini and the rest of the brilliant Penguin team: Nancy Paulsen, Erin Dempsey, Lisa DeGroff, Courtney Wood, Jillian Laks, Scottie Bowditch, RasShahn Johnson-Baker, Kim Lauber, Shauna Fay and Jessica Kaufman. And I definitely can't forget my sales guys: Mary-Margaret Callahan, Allan Winebarger, Holly Ruck, Jackie Engel, Ev Taylor, John Dennany, Biff Donavon, Sheila Hennesey, Doni Kay, Todd Jones, Nicole White, Alex Genis, Colleen Conway, Jill Bailey, Steve Kent, Nicole Davies, Annie Hurwitz, Mary Raymond, Donna Peterson and Jana Fruh. I, more than anyone, know how important you all are to the success of any book. I'm a lucky author to have mine in your hands.

Thanks again to Christopher Moore and Meg Cabot for being unbelievably kind. My appreciation also goes to Stephen Dafoe for his support and encouragement. My colleagues Elise Howard, Lisa Gallagher, Liate Stehlik, Carrie Kania, Mike Brennan, Josh Marwell, Brian Murray and Carla Parker, I couldn't do it without you, and I wouldn't want to try.

Thanks to my wife, Kelly, for doing everything. All the time. Without fail. My son, Mick, of whom I couldn't be prouder, and my daughter, Rachel, who is an inspiration to everyone who meets her for even five seconds. Thanks to my mom, Vi Spradlin, for mom-type support, and my sisters, Regina and Connie, for sister-type encouragement. I love you all so much.

# PROLOGUE

The room was full of bright light with a glare so intense that I closed my eyes. A long table draped in a pure white linen cloth sat in the middle of the room. In the center of the table sat the Grail. It was out of my reach, and having it so far away made me nervous.

Sir Thomas sat quietly at the far end of the table, dressed in his familiar white tunic with a bright red cross across his chest. Smiling, he bade me to sit in a chair next to me. I sat.

Sir Thomas spoke. "You've done well, lad."

I snorted.

"Sire, I have failed. Completely. I did what you asked. I made it safely to Tyre and found a ship, but a storm rose up, and now I have drowned and the Grail is lost with me," I said, bowing my head, ashamed to have disappointed him.

"Tristan?"

I looked up.

"You've not failed me. The Grail is safe, as you can see," he said.

Glancing at the chalice on the table, I shook my head, knowing

I should not be in this room. I was drowning in the sea, and the Grail would perish with me. How could Sir Thomas say I had not failed? The only thing worse would have been for Sir Hugh to have taken it from me.

"Sir Thomas, I have no idea how I came to be here, but this is not right. The Grail has sunk to the bottom of the sea, and me with it. I am sorry, sire. Very truly sorry."

He smiled and the white light of the room surrounded him. I heard a familiar humming sound, but now, instead of coming from the Grail, the noise surrounded me from all directions.

"Do not worry, lad," Sir Thomas said. "You are safe. The Grail is safe."

"Sire . . . ," I replied, but Sir Thomas was no longer there, just the light and the sound.

My chair was gone and I was standing again, the Grail still in the center of the table. I grasped at it, but it remained out of reach. Sir Thomas now appeared beside me, holding a bucket of water in his hands. He said nothing, but dumped the bucket over my head, causing me to choke and sputter.

"Sir Thomas . . . what . . . ," but he was gone again.

The room shifted and I was thrown to the floor. Sir Thomas stood above me with another bucket of water. This time he threw it directly in my face and I swallowed a great deal of it. It tasted salty. When I looked up again, Sir Thomas was gone.

What had happened to me? Why didn't he help me? I needed to reach the Grail and he was interfering. Was this some kind of test? Had I failed again?

I struggled to my feet, but the room was unsteady, as if some giant had picked it up and delighted in shaking it about. I lurched across the floor and crashed into the table. The Grail wobbled back and forth. Oh no.

In vain I tried to clamor forward. If I could reach it, I would secure it in my satchel where it would be safe until I figured a way out of this room. Then I would find the giant shaking it and slay it with my sword.

As suddenly as it started, the room ceased its tossing about. Sir Thomas was back, this time holding the Grail out to me.

"Good luck, Tristan," he said. I took the cup in my hands, clutching it to my chest.

He was gone. The room was gone. Only the bright white light remained.

What had become of me?

# The Southern Coast of France
## October 1191

# I

wall of ocean pushed me beneath the surface. I fought my way up into the air as the water rose and twisted violently, and tried to remember where I was. The tossing of the ship had swept me into the sea. I had no idea how long I'd been in the water but recalled seeing the broken mast come hurtling toward me. But I could remember nothing else. Over the sound of the wind I thought I heard Robard screaming, but it sounded faint and far away. Also, I tasted blood in my mouth.

The moon was completely obscured by the storm clouds. It was so dark that I couldn't see anything. As I came to my senses, I was completely disoriented by the sensation of the angry sea rising and falling. I could not tell up from down. I only knew I was wet. And frankly, a little tired of it all.

Bursting through the water's surface, I sucked in fresh air and felt for the satchel around my neck and shoulder, relieved to find it still there. The rushing sound of water behind me rose again, and I hollered out a curse. But the water was on me now, and I dipped violently in the trough before the wave threw me into the air. I hit the water on my back with a smack, and the breath was pushed from my lungs.

Another wave carried me up and then dashed me down again, and I collided with something hard. At first I thought it was a rock, but when the wave subsided, my feet touched the sea bottom. More waves crashed into me, but when they returned to the sea, I could stand. I didn't know which way to turn in the darkness with the howling wind and rain pelting my face. But then, as if God wanted to give me a fighting chance (or else keep me alive a bit longer to further torment me later), a flash of lightning flickered across the sky, and in a brief instant I saw land ahead of me: a shoreline, with trees and rocks in the distance.

Shouting in glee, I scrambled in the direction the lightning had shown me, the water growing shallower with each step, and before long it reached only my waist, then knees. With every last ounce of strength I splashed forward until the sand was under me, and I collapsed to the ground.

I woke to the taste of sand. It was salty and gritty, and light was coming from somewhere. Where were Robard and Maryam and the dog? Why couldn't I see them? But then I couldn't really see well at all, as my eyes were full of sand. I blinked to clear them and only partially succeeded.

It was relaxing to lie so peacefully, but I made the mistake of trying to lift my head, and the world spun away from me. I sank into unconsciousness.

When I came to again, I was no longer moving, but was still very wet.

Opening my right eye, I wiggled my fingers, delighted to see that they worked. I'm not sure how much more time passed before I tried to move additional body parts. I clenched a fist. No pain.

Sore everywhere, I drove my fist into the sand, lifting myself up on one arm. It was daytime now, and the sun was high in the sky, so it must have been nearly noon. There was a line of trees about two hundred yards farther inland.

Pushing myself up to my hands and knees, I winced when pain shot through my left knee. I had a vague recollection of hitting it on something the night before while thrashing about in the waves. My right elbow also throbbed, but didn't feel broken. When the dizziness passed, I finally stood.

My back wouldn't straighten all the way, and I wondered if my ribs were broken. I looked at the now calm sea. There was no indication of the fury it had unleashed on me the previous night.

Looking up and down the beach, I could see only a league or so in each direction before the shoreline bent out of sight.

"Robard! Maryam!" I shouted, but no one answered. Only the squawk of a few shorebirds disturbed the quiet.

"Captain Denby!"

"Little Dog!" Nothing. No answering bark.

With every intention of walking along the beach, I stumbled to the ground after a few steps, too tired to go any farther. Dropping on the sand, I quickly fell asleep.

When I woke, there were six people standing around me. Two of them were young women, four were men. Each held a horse by the reins.

All of them were pointing swords at me.

hey stood silently, swords in hand, studying me intently. I was unbelievably sore, but tried to make a quick assessment of my situation. Lying on my back, Sir Thomas' battle sword dug into my spine. Good; I hadn't lost it. The satchel was still around my shoulder. I could also feel my belt and the weight of my short sword. I had fought Mother Nature and clearly lost, but I was lucky I wasn't injured more seriously.

Of course, it wasn't "lucky" to be surrounded by sword-wielding strangers. I tried to rise, but a stern look from the woman holding her sword against my neck persuaded me to lie back down.

After a while, the silence became uncomfortable.

"Hello," I said.

Nothing: only more stern looks and sword pointing.

"Nice day. You wouldn't happen to know exactly where we are, would you? I'm very lost."

The young woman who held her sword closest to my neck said something in a language I recognized. French. Brother Rupert was from France and had taught me to speak it a little. By no means was I fluent, but I should be able to communicate. Then I wondered if I was actually *in* France, or had washed ashore some-where else and these French travelers had happened across me.

The others sheathed their swords, but she kept hers out. Not as close to my neck but still at the ready if needed.

"*Je m'appelle* Tristan," I said. I am called Tristan.

"I speak English," she said with just a hint of an accent. "Who are you?"

"Am I in France?" I asked, ignoring her question, compelled to find out where I was.

Sword woman nodded.

"My name is Tristan of St. Alban's. I was attached to a Templar regimento in Outremer, but I am . . . was on my way back to England. Our ship was lost in the storm, and I washed up on this shore. You speak French. Am I in France?" I asked again.

She paused before speaking but nodded. Then she and her companions began an intense conversation that went far too fast for me to understand. I could pick out only a few words here and there, but the tone was heated, and from what I could gather, the others would be happy to kill me or leave me behind and ride on. So I concentrated on the girl with the sword.

I looked past the weapon to her face and realized she was quite beautiful. Her dark hair hung to her shoulders and was pulled back with a headband. Her eyes were a fierce light blue, and her skin was tanned. She had an air of leadership about her, and there was a determined set to her expression. My immediate fate rested in her hands. She looked about my age, and though the rest of her party was older, she was definitely the one in charge.

"A Templar regimento, you say?" she asked.

"Yes."

"We have no love for the Templars, servants of their cowardly Pope," she said. One of her companions, an extremely large and angry-looking man, spat on the ground at the word *Templar*, reminding me of Robard whenever Richard the Lionheart's name was mentioned.

Drat. I silently cursed my big mouth.

"I wouldn't know. I'm only a squire, and have never even met the Pope, so I'm not one to judge his level of bravery," I said.

For a brief instant a very slight smile flashed across her face. The second young woman spoke quietly to the men, and when she did, they cursed and shook their swords excitedly in my direction.

"Yes, well, I can assure you of his cowardice," she said.

I nodded in agreement. No need to try to debate the angry young Frenchwoman.

"I don't want any trouble. If it weren't for the storm, I wouldn't be here at all. All I wish is to find a way home. If you can tell me where we are and the nearest port where I may find a ship, I'll be on my way. May I stand?"

She backed up a few steps and nodded, and I slowly rose to my feet. I groaned with the effort and flexed my knee several times, trying to work the soreness out of it.

"You are injured," she said.

"Not seriously, I don't think," I replied.

"How long were you in the water?"

"I don't know. Since sometime last evening. The mast gave way during the storm and I was thrown into the water, which is the last thing I remember. I have no idea if the ship survived. There were two other passengers and four crewmen, and I fear they may be lost. Oh, you haven't come across a small golden-colored dog, have you?"

She shook her head. "We spotted you from the trees as we rode by. We've seen no one else. Did you hear a humming noise?" she asked.

My skin prickled immediately.

"Noise?"

"Yes. Faint and far away. Sort of a strange musical quality? I heard it when we first saw you, but it stopped when you woke," she said.

She had heard the sound of the Grail. But how?

My vision had narrowed and I thought I might fall to the ground again. If she had heard it, did this mean others had as well? If this were true, then how could I keep it safe?

"No, I heard nothing. In fact, I think my ears are still full of water," I said, willing myself to speak slowly and methodically. Steady, I told myself, looking up at the sky, then down at the sand, then out at the water, trying to be casual. I made another show of flexing my knee and bending my back, trying to make it obvious that I didn't know anything about strange noises.

"My name is Celia," she said, sheathing her sword. I relaxed a little, but not much.

"Can you ride?" she asked.

"I think so," I replied. I looked around but saw no other horses. "Um. But you have six riders for six horses."

"I know. You'll ride behind me."

Ride behind her? No, thank you. She had already said she didn't like Templars, and she was well armed. I'd be safer walking.

"I'd rather walk," I said.

"If you walk, you won't be able to keep up. You'll get lost."

"Then if you'll just point me in the right direction . . ."

She stopped. "You are unable to ride then?"

"No. I can ride. . . . I just . . . I don't . . . I mean," I stammered.

"So then you are uncomfortable sharing the horse with me?"

"What? No, of course not! It's just . . . I mean . . . I'm quite dirty and . . ."

"Would you rather ride with Philippe?" she interrupted, and pointed to the largest of the four men accompanying her. The spitter. He was wearing a purple shirt with the sleeves rolled up, showing off his massive forearms. I imagined Philippe spending many, many hours lifting heavy objects or perhaps crushing rocks with his bare hands. Not to mention how he glowered at me with a look saying that if it were up to him, he'd prefer bashing in my head and leaving me where I'd been found.

"Ah, no," I said.

"You should know, then, that Philippe believes you might be a spy. I haven't decided yet. But since we have the swords, don't you think it best if you come with us? At least until we can decide what to do with you?"

"I have a sword," I said defensively, having been caught completely off guard. I wanted to prove to them that a Templar squire is no one to be trifled with.

"Yes. I see. Two, in fact. We have six."

She had a point.

Done with the discussion, Celia mounted her horse. She nudged him forward and held her hand out to me.

Reluctantly, I grabbed it and struggled up into the saddle behind her.

So far, France did not have much to recommend it.

# 3

e rode west along the beach for several hours without a word passing between us. As dusk approached, Celia rode farther inland toward the tree line. Soon we were riding through the wooded countryside. I hoped we'd find a place to stop shortly, as it was enormously uncomfortable riding the horse. I had overestimated my condition; each hoofbeat brought jarring pain, and every so often a groan escaped my lips. It grew worse when we crossed from the sand onto the more uneven terrain of the forest.

"Are you sure you aren't hurt?" Celia asked.

"No, I'm fine, really," I said through gritted teeth.

Celia chuckled, and then as if to intentionally vex me, slapped the reins and broke into a quick gallop. After a few yards, I couldn't take it anymore and begged her to stop. This only made her spur the horse harder, and after we jumped a small creek, she pulled up into a clearing.

"Are you all right, Templar?" she asked.

With great care, I slid off the horse, nearly tumbling to the ground. With hands on my knees, I struggled to breathe, but each gasp only brought more pain.

"Just need a little rest, but I don't want to hold you up. If you'll just tell me where I can find the nearest port, I'll sleep for a day or three and proceed on my own."

"We're stopping here for the night anyway. Here is fresh water. Philippe should be able to find us something to eat," she said.

By now the other riders in the party had caught up to us. The other young woman and three of the men dismounted and began making preparations to camp for the night. Philippe spoke to Celia in low tones. It was impossible to hear what they were saying, but from their expressions it looked like an argument. She raised her voice at one point, and he glowered in my direction before riding off into the woods. The other members of her group paid no attention to their little spat.

In a matter of minutes, the horses had been tethered between two trees, their saddles removed. A small fire was built in short order, and two of the men scoured the nearby woods for more firewood.

The woman pulled a few cooking implements from a bag she had carried on her saddle. She knelt near the fire, adding more wood.

Still sore, I limped to a nearby tree, slowly lowering myself to the ground and leaning back against the trunk. Sleep came instantly. The clattering sound of Philippe returning woke me. It was still light, but the twilight shadows crept through the forest. Philippe dismounted, carrying some type of large fowl across his saddle. He handed it to one of the men, who left the clearing to clean the bird.

Celia was circling the camp, her hand on the hilt of her sword as if she'd been keeping watch.

"Feeling better?" she asked when she saw me awake.

"Yes, thank you," I said.

"We'll have food soon. Philippe is an excellent hunter, and Martine is an even better cook."

Looking at Philippe, I saw no evidence of a bow or other hunting weapon.

"How does he hunt with no bow?" I asked.

"He has his ways."

Wonderful. I was already on unfriendly terms with a large, enormously strong man with a sword who evidently captured wild game with his bare hands. My situation was improving by the hour. Using the tree for support, I clawed my way to my feet. My back and knee felt better, but I resigned myself to several days of pain and stiffness.

The fowl was cleaned and mounted on a wooden spit. Martine took some herbs from her bag and sprinkled them over the bird, then propped it over the fire. The sight of the food made my stomach growl in anticipation.

Celia smiled and walked to the fire. As I followed her with my eyes, I caught Philippe glaring at me. He had pulled his sword from his scabbard and was sharpening it with a stone. As he worked, he periodically ran his thumb along the edge, never taking his eyes off me.

I smiled and gave him a jaunty wave.

"*Bonjour, mon frère,*" I said.

He was not amused. His eyes darkened and his jaw muscles clenched. It was quite possible he might jump across the fire and thrash me, but he returned to his sword. Then his head snapped up and he hissed, catching everyone's attention. They were on their feet in an instant, silently drawing their swords.

The woods were quiet. Too quiet. Unsure what was going on, I was afraid to pull my own weapon from my belt, lest the friendly Philippe misinterpret it as a threatening move. Something was wrong.

Philippe slowly rotated, looking intently into the woods surrounding our camp. He cocked his head to the side, like a dog searching the underbrush for vermin. He stood about five yards away from me when without warning an arrow thunked into the trunk of the tree between us. Gray goose feathers were attached to the shaft, and I recognized it instantly.

Robard.

# 4

hilippe shouted out a command, and in a blur one of the men kicked dirt over the fire, dousing the flame. He let out a bloodcurdling scream and charged into the brush in the direction the arrow had come from. The other three men melted into the forest.

"Wait!" I shouted. "Robard, don't shoot! These are friends!"

Robard didn't answer, and when I turned to explain to Celia what was happening, I was startled by the sight of Maryam holding Celia firmly from behind with one golden dagger at her neck.

Oh no.

"Maryam, wait! Stop. Everyone stop."

Celia was not moving but cursing rapidly. Maryam ordered her to drop her sword. Celia shouted something back and reluctantly complied.

"Maryam, let her go! For God's sake, she's a friend. These people have not harmed me!"

Maryam looked confused, but did not release her grip on Celia. I heard Robard shout, "Tristan, run! I have you covered!"

"No! Robard, stop! Please put down your bow! And watch out! You have a very large, angry Frenchman headed your way."

"What?" he shouted back.

"Just don't shoot anyone. I'll explain everything. Come into the camp!"

Maryam still held Celia, but in the seconds I'd been preoccupied, Martine had advanced toward her, sword at the ready.

"Martine, *s'il vous plaît. Arrête!*" She ignored me, swinging her sword up. Maryam crouched slightly, then shoved Celia away. She stumbled the few feet between us before falling into my arms.

"No!" I shouted. Martine's sword flashed down, but the Assassin was ready. She crossed both golden daggers over her head, catching the blade of Martine's weapon between them. With blinding speed, she twisted them to the side and the sword was ripped loose.

Pushing Celia back to her feet, I ran between them, holding up my hands against the now advancing Maryam.

"Maryam, stop. It's all right!"

"Tristan! You are alive! Praise Allah! Robard and I are here to rescue you!" she shouted.

"Maryam, I don't need rescuing! These people are helping me. They found me washed up on the beach. Please! Stop this! Before someone gets hurt or killed. Put your weapons away."

Maryam's eyes darted between me, Celia and Martine. She crouched, tense like a coiled spring, and I was torn between enormous joy at finding her alive and extreme worry that something horrible was going to happen. Robard was also in grave danger. There were four Frenchmen in the woods who didn't know these attackers were not enemies.

"Celia, these are my companions from the boat. They made a mistake and mean you no harm. They incorrectly believed me to be a prisoner. Please! Tell your men to stand down!"

Celia looked from me to Maryam and was still angry at being held at knifepoint.

"If one of my men is injured by your bowman, I will hold you responsible, Templar!" she said. But she shouted out to the men, and the woods went quiet again. After what felt like an eternity the three men returned to the clearing. All but Philippe.

"Robard, if you can hear me, you need to put away your bow! These people found me washed up on the shore this morning. They've been helping me. Please! Come into the clearing so we can all discuss this!"

No sound came from the woods. Then from the underbrush, there came a yelp and the sounds of a scuffle. Next, a shouted curse in English, followed by one in French.

The men in the camp were still ready to fight at any second, holding their swords unsheathed.

"Celia, please tell Philippe to stop," I begged.

"Sorry, Templar," she replied. "When Philippe is in a rage, there is little I or anyone can do to control him."

Philippe and Robard emerged from a thicket thirty yards beyond the camp. They were grappling with each other, but I could tell they were both tiring. Robard had his hands around Philippe's throat, but the big Frenchman clubbed his arms away. He threw a wild punch, but Robard ducked it easily, jumping on Philippe's back when his momentum carried him around. Philippe tried to flip him off and finally caught Robard by the hair, tossing him forward through the air.

Robard landed hard on his back and lay stunned on the ground. Philippe pulled a small dagger from his belt.

Celia and I both shouted, but Philippe behaved as if he did not hear us. Robard had rolled to his hands and knees, but his back was to the Frenchman. Maryam started toward Robard's side, shouting, but two of Celia's men moved threateningly toward her and I put out my arm to stop her, not wanting this to get any worse than it already was.

Philippe was only a few feet from Robard when a golden streak whirled past me, headed directly toward the Frenchman, barking furiously. It was the dog.

Unafraid of Philippe's great size, she ran full speed at him and leapt into the air, clamping down on his wrist with her jaws.

He shook his wrist, howling in pain, but she would not let go. He dropped the dagger and danced around the clearing shrieking, but could not free his arm. Robard finally rose and shouted a command, and she instantly released her grip. She didn't retreat though, backing up a few steps and going low to the ground, growling, muscles coiled and teeth bared. The fight had finally gone out of both Robard and Philippe, who stood eyeing each other.

Seizing the moment, I moved between them, holding out my arms.

"Both of you, stop! Enough! There are no enemies here. Robard, I am very glad you are alive, but this has been a mistake. I am not a prisoner."

Robard was still confused and dazed by his fight with Philippe. He was out of breath, but I wanted him to calm down. There was no need to make enemies when we were outnumbered and in a strange land.

Imagine my surprise, then, when I looked back to find Celia and her companions pointing at the mutt at my feet and laughing hysterically.

elia, Martine and the others were laughing wildly now. Philippe and Robard looked at us, perplexed. Maryam stared at them in wonder, but lowered her daggers.

"Oh. Oh my goodness," Celia said, wiping at her eyes, trying to control her laughter. "Philippe! You have been undone by a savage beast!" She chuckled again, and Martine and the rest of her group joined in.

"Celia? Philippe still looks ready to charge. Can you please ask him to relax?"

Celia tried but burst out laughing again. Although Philippe had temporarily stopped his advance on Robard, the dog sat on her haunches barking excitedly, then jumped up and down until I scooped her up in my arms. She licked my face, and this brought another round of laughter.

"Celia?" I asked.

Celia spoke to Philippe and he answered back sharply. She talked over him until, with one last glare at Robard, he stormed off toward the stream, washing his hands and face in the water, complaining loudly all the time.

"Friendly fellow," Robard said, still trying to catch his breath.

Celia's head snapped around to face Robard, and her eyes blazed. She had gone from laughter to anger in a heartbeat.

"We do not appreciate being shot at for no reason. Someone could have been killed," Celia replied. There was steel in her voice, and given Robard's temper, I knew this could start things up again.

Robard looked surprised she could understand him. To avoid her intense gaze he occupied himself with straightening his tunic and slapping the dust and dirt out of his breeches.

"Mademoiselle, I assure you: if I wanted someone dead, they'd be dead. It was a warning shot, a diversion to give Maryam a chance to act. It appeared you were holding my friend prisoner," he said.

I interrupted, hoping to change the subject and defuse the situation.

"Robard, where did you come from? How did you survive the storm? How did you find me? Us? And where is your bow?"

Truth be told, I still didn't know much about Celia and her group. They had yet to show me anything other than a sort of abrupt kindness, but they still made me wary. Considering we were outnumbered, I thought it best that Robard remain armed.

"We followed your tracks from the beach. The boat broke apart, but we managed to cling to a piece of the decking and were blown ashore. We found a set of footprints on the beach, thinking it might be someone from the ship, then discovered six riders had surrounded whoever made them. In the woods where the Frenchman knocked it out of my hand," he replied dutifully.

"And with such paltry information you decided it was necessary to attack us?" Celia snorted. She was not easily pushed off point.

Robard looked at her and smiled.

"My mistake, mademoiselle. Please accept my apologies," he said, bowing gallantly.

Maryam sheathed her daggers and gave me a hug so fierce I thought it might push all the breath from my lungs.

"Tristan, are you hurt?" she asked.

"I wasn't," I groaned at the intensity of her embrace, which had reawakened the aches and pains I'd suffered in the shipwreck. Finally her hands rested on my upper arms, and she looked me up and down. Celia studied Maryam intently. Forgetting her anger with Robard, her face clouded as she watched Maryam inspect me.

"No, Maryam. I'm just sore from being battered about by the waves. I'm fine. Really."

"Praise Allah!" Maryam said.

It took a few minutes of explanations and questions back and forth until everyone was satisfied. Celia introduced everyone in her troop, but Philippe sulked off near the horses by himself. Once Celia had explained everything, they were willing to let bygones be bygones, all of them smiling and having another good laugh over the dog so ferociously attacking Philippe.

"*Mon dieu*, that was funny," Celia said. "Poor Philippe. Such a vicious little creature!" The dog jumped down from my arms and twirled at Celia's feet, barking happily. Celia scooped her up and rubbed her ears and muzzle. Traitorous cur!

"How adorable," she said. The dog licked her face. "What a sweet little angel. What is her name?"

"Her name? I . . . uh . . . Her name . . . It's . . . her name . . ."

"You don't know the name of your own dog?" she asked.

"I haven't had her very long . . . ," I stammered.

"How long?" Celia demanded.

"Not . . . since we left Tyre a few days ago . . . really . . . She just tagged along . . . and . . ."

"And you haven't given her a *name?*" She was incredulous. "Poor little thing." She smiled and cooed, "Sweet little angel."

"Of course she has a name! It's . . . um . . . Angel. Her name is Angel!" I said.

Celia arched an eyebrow in disbelief. I held her gaze.

"It certainly fits," she said, giggling as "Angel" resumed attempting to lick her to death.

"What happened to Captain Denby and the crew?" I asked Robard, wanting to change the subject from my poor stewardship of the newly christened Angel.

"Lost, I would expect." He shrugged. "His sorry excuse for a ship came apart like parchment. There were no signs of other survivors on the shore except your tracks. We're lucky the wind blew us all in the same direction. We completely lost sight of you when you went into the water."

Robard's words caused me to shudder at the memory. Once we located another ship and made it safely to England, ideally my sailing days would be over. If only there were a way for me to walk all the way home. What I wouldn't have given for a bridge to England.

"I'm glad you are unhurt and we are all together again," I said. And it was true. Finding Maryam and Robard here had done wonders for my spirits. My aches and pains even felt better.

The fire was restarted, and the bird was again cooking over the flames. One of the other Frenchmen, whom Celia had introduced as Jean-Luc, returned from the nearby woods with several bunches of wild grapes. He offered some to us and we devoured them in seconds. Having had nothing to eat since the storm started a day and half before, I was starving.

After we had finished the deliciously cooked bird, Philippe saddled his horse and rode off into the darkness. We sat around the fire with very little conversation among us. My suspicions were that everyone in Celia's group spoke and understood English, though for some unexplained reason they were loath to let on. My curiosity could wait no longer, and I asked to speak to Celia in private. The flickering firelight lit up the clearing quite well, but her face was still bathed in shadows. The night was clear, but the moon had yet to rise, and through the canopy of trees, I could see the stars lighting their way across the sky.

"Thank you for your hospitality and for your kindness to my friends, despite what happened earlier," I said.

She nodded, her face a mask, though I sensed a change in her. The tension from the evening's earlier excitement had left her.

"That said, I have a question," I said.

She waited silently.

"Who are you?" I asked.

"I beg your pardon?"

"You travel with a group of young men, all well mounted and armed. You are obviously educated, and if I had to guess, I would say you are a noblewoman of some sort. Your men are well trained and experienced in warfare. When Robard shot at us, not a single one of your men panicked, and Philippe, not even knowing what the danger might be, went charging directly at a King's Archer in your defense. Each of them follows your orders to the letter, except for Philippe, of course. Is he some sort of personal bodyguard or military commander? Martine, I would guess, is your lady-in-waiting. So, I ask again, who are you and what are you doing here in the middle of nowhere?"

A veil of caution descended over her face. Then she exhaled slowly.

"You are quite observant, Templar, even when you are half drowned. Tell me, are your 'injuries' a deceit?"

"No," I insisted.

From the fire, the murmur of voices reached us. The three Frenchmen and Martine chatted away happily while Robard and Maryam sat trying to decipher what was being said. Robard had removed his arrow from the tree trunk and worked at repairing it, but his eyes never left the rest of the group.

"Are you in some kind of trouble? Are you being followed?"

"What makes you think so?" she asked.

"You ride single file, to mix your tracks and confuse any pursuers as to your numbers. Your own mount is placed in the middle of the group, with soldiers in front and behind. Philippe takes the lead, and he watches the horizon constantly. And several times today he looked behind us to make sure no one followed. Your choice of this campsite was carefully selected, though you tried to make it appear casual by a mad dash into the woods from the shore. We are placed one side against a stream, so any attackers would need to cross it first if they came from the west. We are also in a small hollow, so the fire will not be easily visible to casual passersby. And if I'm not mistaken, Philippe just made a big show of being sullen over his fight with Robard, but I'm sure it was just an excuse to leave and scout the surrounding countryside. Shall I go on?"

Celia wouldn't look at me. "How has a squire so young learned so much?" she asked.

"For the last year and half I have done nothing but study tactics and train for war. My knight, Sir Thomas, is . . . was . . . a brilliant military mind. He taught me everything. I have seen much."

She said nothing, but I could tell she was trying to decide whether or not to let me in on her secret, whatever it might be.

"Celia, please, maybe I can help you."

She laughed. "This is trouble you don't want, squire."

"Let me be the judge of that."

"You are a kind one, aren't you?"

Something about Celia made me want to tell her things about myself. Things I had never told anyone. It might have been her hair and how it framed her face, or the ice-blue pools of her eyes. Maybe it was the way the firelight danced across her smiling face, making her look mysterious and inviting all at the same time.

These were things I had never noticed in anyone before. Except for the pleasant smell of Maryam's hair and the beautiful sound of her laugh. Was something wrong with me? For some reason, the abbot's face appeared in my head and I felt a sudden urge to pray. Celia was so close to me then. And she smelled like the abbey garden in springtime.

"I hope so. I'd like to think I am, being raised by Cistercian monks. They were men of kindness. I hope I learned something from them," I told her.

She turned back to me, close enough that I could see her lovely face more clearly. "Raised by monks? What happened to your parents?"

"Never knew them. I was left at the abbey as a babe."

"How sad! It must be terrible not knowing who your family is."

I shrugged. "You can't really miss what you've never had. It could have been worse. There was a roof over my head and food to eat. Many orphans have probably not met so kind a fate. Please stop trying to change the subject."

"Do you always put others before yourself, Templar? Is this a trait you learned at your abbey?"

"I don't know."

Her gaze traveled back to the fire, to study her people. "We are Cathars."

She looked at me expectantly to see what effect her words had on me. But I had no idea what a Cathar was. She went on.

"We live not far from here, in the mountain towns of the Pyrenees. My father is the bishop of our canton. I think you English might call it a county. Cathars are no friends to the church. We believe in tolerance of other religions and that all the trappings of the church are . . . irrelevant and only get in the way of a true connection with God. Still, despite our objections to how the church is run, we have lived in peace for many years, but now, things are different. We allow anyone to worship as they please, but your Pope has a much dimmer view of Catharism," she said.

Having lived in a monastery most of my life, I knew the Bible somewhat, but I was no religious scholar. For a time, I had a natural curiosity about the monks and their unwavering allegiance to God. But I had never felt the pull of their devotion. I prayed. I believed. But I did not know what to say to Celia, not understanding very much of what she said.

"So because the Pope is angry with your people, you are hiding here in the woods?"

Celia laughed.

"No, Templar. We are not hiding. My father sent me to counsel with emissaries of the Archbishop of Languedoc while he travels to Paris to seek an audience with King Philip. Our message grows. We have more followers now. This upsets your Pope. The archbishop demanded our presence before him immediately. My father cares little for what the archbishop demands, but also knows he can be a powerful enemy. Since Father could not be in two places at once, he sent me to Narbonne in his stead. He wanted me to attempt to appease the archbishop if I could, but I am afraid I only managed to anger him."

"Anger him? How?" I asked.

"I'm not sure. It may have been when I called him a fat, pretentious, overbearing cow," she said, shrugging.

"That would do it," I said. This was all very strange to me. At St. Alban's the brothers managed to stay far removed from church politics. I remember a bishop visiting once when I was younger. And I remember the abbot being ill tempered for weeks after, but I couldn't recall there ever being any other problems. Of course, I'm certain the abbot would never call the bishop a cow either. This may have had more to do with Celia's predicament than a difference in theology.

"We were on our way home when we found you," she went on. "The conference did not go well, especially after my outburst. The archbishop made many threats. Philippe believes he will move against us before my father can even gain an audience with the King. He may have sent soldiers after us, so Philippe is just being cautious."

"Why do they care what you do if you bother no one?"

"You *must* have grown up in an abbey, to ask such an incredibly naïve question. The church does as it will. It is not the kings and monarchs who rule us, but Pope Celestine III. Does not your own order answer only to him?"

"Yes. I suppose, but I . . ."

"He has decided the Cathars are enemies of the church, Templar. And now we must decide what to do about it, which is why Philippe is so upset with me. He thinks we should have left you on the beach. He feels we should be well on our way to Montségur by now instead of taking you to the nearest port."

"Montségur?"

"It is our fortress in the mountains. When we are threatened, we retreat there for safety. Usually whoever is upset with us at the moment lays siege, but eventually gives up and leaves. However, Philippe is certain there will be a greater threat this time. As my father's Seneschal, he wishes to return there at once, but he swore an oath to follow my command."

"Maybe you should listen to him. Grateful as I am to you for not hurting my friends in their misguided attempt to rescue me, we are well able to find the port on our own, and you can resume your journey."

Celia did not have a chance to respond, for just then Philippe rode hurriedly into camp and hastily dismounted.

*"On arrive!"* he said.

"What did he say?" I asked.

"Someone is coming," Celia said.

# 6

hilippe and Celia spoke rapidly. Philippe barked orders, and his men immediately broke camp. Each of them spun off from the fire to an assigned duty.

"What is happening?" Robard asked. He and Maryam rose from the fire.

"I'm not sure. There is some kind of trouble. I think someone is after them."

Robard looked at me in disbelief, then snorted. "What do you mean by *trouble* exactly?"

"What other kind of trouble do we know?" I asked.

The fire was extinguished and we were plunged into darkness. The half moon had just peeked over the horizon, and there was enough light for me to see Robard's face.

"Just to be sure, you mean the bad-men-chasing-us-again kind?" he asked.

"Yes, I'm afraid so," I said apologetically.

Robard sighed. "I will say this. Since I rescued you from those bandits, you've never been at a shortage for excitement."

"Tristan, what are we going to do?" Maryam asked.

"Celia and her group are being pursued by enemies of some sort. She calls herself a Cathar, whatever that means." Robard and Maryam shrugged. "Her father is an important religious leader among her people and has made enemies of the church. An archbishop they met with in a place called Narbonne is angry with them for some reason. Philippe was convinced they were followed, and now he has spotted something."

"Something?" Robard asked. He knew the answer. Danger was approaching.

"This is not our concern. You don't intend to become involved in her problems, do you?" Maryam asked.

"No, I don't plan to," I said.

In truth, I had no idea what to do. Did I owe anything to Celia? I had my duty to the Grail to consider. If they were being pursued by a large force, their only logical choice was flight. Robard, Maryam and I could slip away into the forest and work our way toward the coast and follow it until we came upon a port.

Within minutes, the horses were saddled and nearly every sign of our camp was gone. Only a close inspection by an experienced forester would find any evidence that a camp had ever been made here.

Celia approached the three of us while her friends mounted their horses.

"Philippe says nearly fifty of the archbishop's guards are tracking us. They are a few miles back and moving slowly, but will be on us before morning if we do not leave right away." She looked at me expectantly.

"Then you must leave now," I said.

"What will you do?" she asked.

"We'll be fine; we'll head back toward the shore and follow it west until we find a port city. Don't worry about us," I told her.

Celia looked down at the ground for a moment, as if struggling to speak.

"Tristan, realize this: these men following us are ruthless. They kill and maim with no provocation. If they suspect you have seen us and helped us in any way . . ." She let the words hang in the air.

"We'll be safe," I assured her.

"How do you know . . . ?" She looked at me strangely, but I nodded. The Grail had kept me safe thus far. It would protect the three of us. Then, almost as if she remembered how the strange sound she had heard pulled her to me on the beach, she nodded. I hadn't had much time to think about it, but I wondered if the Grail was pulling me to her just as much. As if she needed its protection as well. But that sounded foolish. My duty was to protect the Grail, not to treat its wonders like a cheap carnival trick. Sir Thomas had entrusted it to me because he believed I would keep it safe. And although I sorely wished he had picked someone else, he had chosen me. I had to get on with my mission.

"You are a two-day walk from Perpignan. You should easily find a ship there," she said.

Philippe was mounted and impatient to be under way. "Mademoiselle . . . ," he whispered.

"Shh," she hissed at him.

"Thank you, Tristan," she said.

"For what?" I asked.

"For listening." She nodded good-bye to Maryam and Robard, then mounted her horse, and we watched in silence as they rode away into the darkness.

Robard had retrieved his bow and held it in his left hand. Nervously shifting back and forth on his feet, he coughed quietly.

"Tristan?" he asked.

"Yes?"

"Time to go," he said.

Both Maryam and Robard were eager to be on their way. We started off at a trot, following the stream. It would lead us to the shore eventually, and from there we could make our way to the city. We hiked in the opposite direction of Celia and her riders. Moving along in silence, Robard finally suggested we stop for the night.

"We need to rest," he said. "I'm exhausted. Haven't had much sleep since we came out of the water."

"All right," I said. "But we should reach the shore soon. We should make camp there. We'll be far enough away from Celia's camp then. If anyone finds us, it will be easier to convince them we've been following the shore and haven't come across any other travelers."

By the time two hours went by, the half moon rode high in the sky, providing us some light. The smell of salt water wafted over us, and we broke through the trees. There before us was the shore. It gave me pause to look again upon the ocean that had spit me out not so long ago. I took no joy in being near the water again.

We weren't hungry, but we built a fire, and its light and warmth did much to improve my mood. No one spoke much; we were all too tired to talk. Angel found a spot close to the fire, curled up and was soon fast asleep.

It was time for me to carefully examine the contents of my satchel, and I was pleased to see that everything, although damp, had survived with little damage. On the second day aboard ship I'd wrapped Sir Thomas' letter and the note I brought from the abbey in oilskin to protect them from the dampness. They were wet, but both were still readable and would likely dry out in fine shape. Even my blue woolen blanket had made it through.

With Maryam and Robard close by I couldn't inspect the Grail, but Robard had shot an arrow through the satchel at very close range when we were back in Outremer and it had survived without a scratch. The Grail had likely survived being bounced about in the waves. I would check on it later, when I had time alone.

Staring at the flames, I worried about Celia, remembering how I had been followed by the King's Guards in Dover. They had shadowed me through the marketplace and had taken some strange interest in me. I had no idea what they wanted. But they acted with impunity. Powerful men like kings and archbishops always had plenty of soldiers and thieves to do their bidding. It wasn't fair.

The fire helped me relax, and I realized how tired I was. Maryam was stifling yawns as well. Robard volunteered to take the first watch, so I lay down next to the fire and closed my eyes, asleep in seconds.

Robard shook me awake a few hours later. He had banked the coals and the fire glowed. The warmth was comforting in the chill of the night as I held my hands over it, still feeling groggy and sore, and wincing at any movement of my still aching muscles.

Instead of keeping a sharp eye for anyone who came our way, I squatted close to the fire and closed my eyes for a few minutes. In my dream, the humming sound of the Grail came to me again. It pulled me up from the darkest depths of sleep, and when my eyes opened, its song was replaced by Angel's low growl. Maryam and Robard were still asleep, but it was nearly daybreak. Scrambling to my knees, I searched the surrounding woods, feeling like I had just awoken from a bad dream. Angel snarled again, louder this time, and stood, teeth bared, staring into the darkness.

"*Bonjour,*" a voice said quietly from behind me.

I jumped in the air and my hand clutched the hilt of my sword as I spun around.

There on the beach a few yards from the fire was a large force of mounted horsemen. They were all dressed in black tunics with gold crosses on the chest. Each of them was heavily armed with sword, lance and shield. At the head of the column rode a very tall, resplendent-looking man wearing the same black tunic but with a golden cape, rimmed with white fur, around his shoulders. His beard was neatly trimmed, and in the gathering light I could see his dark hair and black, cold eyes. He wore a very large ring made of gold on his right hand. He was a priest or monsignor of some rank. Having grown up around monks, I still thought it odd to find a man of God in command of troops. But it was not an uncommon practice. Celia had made mention of an archbishop who was angry with her, and it appeared he had sent his most trusted priest to track her down.

He stared down at me with an expression on his face I couldn't quite place at first, then did. Amusement. He dismounted and strode toward the fire until he stood just a few feet away. Angel did not like his uninvited invasion of our camp. She growled again, moving between me and the stranger.

"Looks to be a ferocious dog. Does he bite?" the man asked.

I nodded.

He chose to ignore Angel, who backed up until her rump rested against my leg. I could feel the tension in her body and had no doubt she would spring in a heartbeat if this man made the wrong move. "You are dressed as a servant of the Templars, are you not?" he asked. He spoke English with a very thick French accent, reminding me of King Richard. But I understood him just fine.

I nodded.

"Do you intend to draw your sword?" he asked, pointing to my hand, which still clutched the hilt of my weapon.

I shook my head. He had yet to give me a reason.

"Good. Are you able to speak?" he asked.

I nodded again, which made him smile.

"Excellent. Then I'm hoping you will be able to help me locate a group of outlaws. I suspect you crossed paths with them last night," he said. His tone said he knew this to be true and it would be useless for me to deny it. He never took his eyes off me.

Without moving my head, I glanced down. Robard's eyes were open and he was looking at me, trying desperately to figure out what to do. His wallet and bow sat leaning against a tree trunk a few inches from his hand.

"Please leave the bow and arrows where they are," the priest said, evidently aware that Robard was awake. There was a lack of menace in his voice, which only made him sound more formidable. He spoke with a casual certainty as if expecting us to obey his commands without question.

Very slowly Robard rose to stand next to me. He yawned, running his hand through his hair as if he wasn't bothered by any of this at all.

"I don't believe we've met," Robard said.

"Then you must allow me to introduce myself," the man replied. "I am the High Counsel to the Archbishop of Languedoc. My men

36

and I are on the trail of six heretics. We followed them to your camp upstream. We lost their trail north of here and then followed your tracks. Now, if you please, I would like to know, where are they headed?"

I had a feeling this High Counsel would not take well to deception.

"Heretics? I thought you said you were on the trail of outlaws," Robard asked.

"One and the same," he replied.

"We need to know which," Robard said. "I have no use for heretics, but outlaws, well, that's a different story. So which is it, Father?"

The High Counsel's eyes narrowed and his face turned to stone. I groaned inwardly. Not now, Robard.

"We had no idea they were heretics, Father," I interrupted before Robard could say anything more. "We were shipwrecked east of here a few days ago. They found us on the beach and offered us food. That's all. I can't say for sure where they were headed, but I heard the word *Perpignan* a few times. Might it be the name of a city or town?"

The High Counsel had locked eyes with Robard while I spoke, but now he looked at me again.

"Perpignan? Yes, it's a nearby city. Are you sure?"

"If it is west of here, it must be where they are headed. When they broke camp, they headed south, riding in the shallows. They must have been trying to hide their tracks from you. They probably turned west downstream."

The High Counsel looked at me, his black eyes never wavering. I don't think he even blinked.

"Why would they head to Perpignan?" he asked, thinking out loud.

"Can't swear to it, Father, as I speak only a little French, just heard them mention it. And they said something about *reserves*. Doesn't that mean 'supplies'? Maybe they needed something there?" I had spun a vast web of deceit now and hoped the High Counsel and his men would leave soon so I could resume breathing.

He studied me, his brow knitted together ever so slightly, then turned and spoke to one of the mounted riders behind him in hushed tones.

"Very well. Thank you for your assistance. We shall ride toward Perpignan and see if we can pick up their trail. If you come across them again, avoid them. They are outcasts and enemies of the church. They have committed grave sins against God," he said.

"Yes, Father. Of course," I said. "May God have mercy on their souls."

He remounted his horse and the column slowly moved westward. He stopped, turning his horse back toward us.

"If I find out you've lied to me, Templar, God will be the only one to grant you mercy."

# 7

hat a rude fellow," said Robard as the High Counsel and his men faded into the distance.

"Who was rude?" Maryam said as she staggered to her feet.

"So glad you could join us. Help us fend off the attackers," Robard teased.

"What are you talking about?" she mumbled.

"We just met Celia's pursuers," I said.

"Nice men, one and all," said Robard.

"What did they want?" Maryam asked.

"They referred to Celia and her band as heretics and outlaws," I told her.

"Actually he said outlaws first and then heretics," Robard pointed out. "Then Tristan told this fellow, who calls himself the High Counsel to some Archbishop of Lancelot, an elaborate fib to throw them off the trail."

"Languedoc, Robard, not Lancelot," I murmured. Robard gave me a dismissive wave and shrugged his wallet onto his back.

Maryam yawned and stretched. In truth the three of us could probably have stood to sleep for several more hours, but I had just told a deliberate lie to a dangerous man who rode at the head of fifty very heavily armed soldiers. It would be best if we were not easily found when he discovered my deceit.

"What are we going to do now?" Maryam asked.

Needing to think, I had unconsciously looked to the north, which led to Celia and her people.

"Oh no. No, Tristan. Absolutely not! I know that look of yours!" Robard stared at me, hands on his hips.

"What look?" I asked innocently.

"The noble and stupid look you get. The one that says you're thinking about going after this Celia to help her," he complained. "You had the same look on your face in Tyre when you jumped into the water to rescue the dog!"

"I do not . . . No . . . I mean, I'm not thinking . . . only . . ." I didn't want to admit it, but the thought of going after Celia had occurred to me. Yet I couldn't ask my friends to take part in something that really did not involve them. I was drawn to Celia, but it was not their concern.

"What are you two talking about?" Maryam cut in.

"He's smitten with the girl. He thinks he can help her or keep this High Counsel fellow from catching up to her. It's not your business, squire. We need to find a ship. I want to get home. This is, if you've not discovered yet, a wretched country. Two of the seven people I've met so far have been quite unpleasant. I want to leave these Franks behind me. The sooner the better."

In the midst of his rant, Robard had grasped the very essence of my dilemma. Despite his bluster and occasional—all right, frequent—poor humor, he did have an uncanny ability to cut through a problem and see it for what it was. How could I ask my

40

friends to delay their journeys while I traipsed after Celia? Besides, I had sent the High Counsel on a wild goose chase, and Celia and her friends were headed in the exact opposite direction. They knew he was coming. What aid could I offer? One more sword, to make it seven against fifty? With any luck they would reach their mountain fortress and get safely away from this man. But what if they did not? What if the High Counsel saw through my ruse and Celia and her group were captured?

On top of it all there was one other argument in Robard's favor. Any time I spent following after Celia or delaying my trip back to England were days that would allow Sir Hugh to catch up to us. As sure as I was of anything, I knew he was coming. I had no doubt he had taken a ship from Tyre and followed us. Sir Hugh was cunning. It would have taken him no time to secure a ship and supplies, and he could have left just a few hours after we had. Until he was sure we were dead or lost in the storm, he wouldn't stop looking.

"What are you thinking?" Maryam asked.

Robard kicked dirt on the fire and grabbed his bow.

"I'm thinking about Sir Hugh," I said.

"What about him?" she asked.

"He will follow us here. He won't just assume we drowned in the storm. Once on shore, he'll go to the nearest commandery and put out word he is searching for us. Maybe even offer a reward. It's not safe for us to find a port anymore."

"Oh? And what would you suggest we do? Walk home?" Robard said.

"Yes," I said.

"You must be joking," Robard said.

I shook my head.

"All right, forget that for an instant. Why would Sir Hugh care so much about a squire?" Robard asked. "If he did follow us, he saw the storm. What would make him keep coming after you? Why wouldn't he assume our rickety ship had sunk, and us with it? What do you have that makes him take after you with such determination?"

Part of me wanted to tell them exactly why. After all this, they'd earned the right to know. But I couldn't forget my pledge to Sir Thomas. The fact that I carried the most sacred relic in all of Christendom must remain my secret. Luckily, for once I had thought ahead and prepared a story.

"Sir Hugh wants power. He wants to be Master of the Order. In Acre, he was accused by Sir Thomas of breaking Templar law. I carry evidence of this, the written testimony of Sir Thomas and a few other knights. If this knowledge becomes known to the current Master, Sir Hugh is finished. This is why he wants me dead. I buried the evidence in the alley in Tyre before we went to the Commandery and retrieved it before we left. I swore to Sir Thomas I would see this duty through. I'm following the last order of my knight."

"Yet in Tyre you only told them Acre was lost. You didn't present your evidence to the Marshal there," Robard said, his eyes narrowing suspiciously.

"I didn't know if he could be trusted. Sir Hugh was already there, and Sir Thomas thought word must be sent to warn the Master alone. And to do so I must return to England."

"So you lied to us?" Maryam interrupted. "You kept the true nature of your mission a secret from us. Why?"

"If we had been caught or Sir Hugh had captured us before we got to Tyre, it was better for you both if you didn't know anything. He is after me, not you. If I'd told you or if he suspected I'd told you, you'd be in even more danger."

I tried hard to confuse them so they wouldn't focus on specifics. I wanted to get moving and leave this discussion behind us. My story was full of holes, and all I could do was make Sir Hugh out to be an evil and manipulative villain and hope they would concentrate on him.

I held my breath. Robard and Maryam were studying me. My gaze never dropped from their eyes. If they demanded to see the evidence I carried, I was safe with Robard, for I knew he could not read. I didn't know about Maryam. She had been born a merchant's daughter, and if she could speak English, she might be able to read it as well. If they wanted proof, I was in trouble. Sir Thomas' letter said nothing about Sir Hugh.

The sun had fully cleared the horizon now and was burning away the early morning mist. We had to get moving. But I waited while Robard and Maryam considered my words.

"So if we accept your story, how do you intend to get to England?" Robard asked skeptically.

"I have thought about this. Since the ports are the first place Sir Hugh will look, I think we go overland, north to the Channel, and get a ship there. It will take him time to search this part of the coast. If we head inland, we can get a head start on him."

"Do you have any idea how long it will take?" Robard snorted. "Weeks, at least! Months even! Not to mention your friend the High Counsel will also be looking for you when he finds out you lied to him. What do you intend to do about him?"

"I intend to hurry." I knelt down, shaking out my blanket and rolling it up. It had been soaked in salt water, and as it dried, had grown stiff, but it still looped over my shoulder easily enough.

"Maryam," I said. "I would like you to come with us. If we can get to London, the Master will make arrangements for you to return to your home on a Templar ship. If you wish to try to find your way alone, I understand."

Maryam looked at me for several seconds. Her face was impassive at first, then changed, and for a brief instant doubt flashed across her features. She didn't believe me. She knew I hadn't told either of them the truth, but didn't challenge me. Since we had first met her, Maryam had argued with Robard repeatedly, but she took me at my word. I wondered why, but had no time to think about it.

After putting the fire out, we were ready to leave. I was hungry and hoped we could find something along the way. Berries or nuts or maybe Robard could shoot some game.

I waited while Maryam washed her face and hands in the stream. She stood looking at me and nodded. She was ready. "All right, Tristan. If you think this is the best approach, I'll go with you."

Robard still stood quietly. I couldn't tell what he was thinking.

"So are you coming with us?" I asked.

Robard looked out at the sea for a second, then at me. "No," he said. "This is good-bye."

aryam looked stricken.

"What? Robard, you can't be serious!" she said.

Robard shook his head as he slung the wallet onto his back and fiddled with the bow's string.

"I'm sorry, Maryam, but I can't. I have duties at home, responsibilities to my father and family. The longer I delay, the greater their burden," he said. Robard sounded sad when he spoke of his family, and for the first time since I'd met him, I realized how much he missed them. I was already guilty of delaying his return. Yet I still needed him.

"Robard, I understand, but you musn't . . ."

Robard held up his hand, shaking his head.

"No, Tristan. Not this time. You are my friend. Aside from being thrown in jail, shot at by crossbows, shipwrecked and wrestling with a large Frenchman, I have enjoyed your company. I even appreciate your sense of duty. But I cannot wait any longer. And if I do, you'll talk me into something again, and before I know it, I'll be hiking through the French countryside dodging who knows whom or what. This is what I need to do."

My shoulders slumped. I wished to tell him the truth and almost did. It was there, right on the tip of my tongue. I would gladly reveal all of my secrets to both of them. But I could not. And I could not deny Robard this.

I stood up straight and held out my hand, and he shook it.

"I owe you much, my friend," I said.

"Try to stay out of trouble," he said. He looked at Maryam and his face softened.

"Good-bye, Maryam. I have enjoyed . . ."

"What are you going to do? How are you going to find a way home? Tristan, will you try to talk some sense into him?" She stormed off a few paces and glared at both of us.

Maryam's reaction confused me. She had done nothing but argue with Robard from the first and now she expected me to persuade him to stay? I had grown up in a monastery, without women. Was this how women acted all the time? They said one thing, yet did another. If so, I now understood the monks a little better.

"His mind is made up, Maryam," I said.

"So un—make up your mind!" she said sharply. "You have a duty to your friend. What kind of soldier are you!"

This was the Maryam I was used to.

"I am no longer a soldier. I have done my duty," he snapped.

"I think you're afraid!" she yelled.

"Afraid? Of what?"

"Of Sir Hugh, of this High Counsel . . ."

Robard held up his hand. "Enough. It's decided. I'm leaving. Good-bye, Tristan. Good luck. I hope we'll meet again. When you reach England, come to Sherwood Forest and look for me. Our farm lies along the eastern edge of the forest, not far from Nottingham."

Without another word he started walking toward the west, following the tracks of the High Counsel and his men.

Angel had remained silent through our exchange but now barked at him.

"Sorry, dog . . . Angel. He's leaving," I said.

She sprinted after Robard and circled his feet, barking and pushing at his legs, trying to drive him back to us.

"What . . . Get down! Stay. Go back!" Robard exclaimed.

But she would not be deterred. She ran back and forth between us, barking madly, but Robard kept walking, and Angel finally returned to us and sat on her haunches, whining pitifully.

Maryam stood silent, glowering at the receding figure. "I hope he's happy with himself," she scoffed.

"Don't be too hard on him, Maryam. His family does need him. Times are hard in England," I said. "Now, if you're coming with me, I think we should get started."

Robard had vanished around the bend, so we headed back the way we had come the night before. Angel waited and waited and finally followed along reluctantly. Both she and Maryam were in foul moods, and Maryam muttered under her breath as we walked. I had the feeling she had no desire for conversation, so I kept silent.

Worried as I was about Maryam, my greatest concern was finding our way to England. We were in a strange country, and I knew only that home lay somewhere to the north. Since I had left the temple in Acre, nothing had happened as I had hoped. Now I was blundering about in a foreign land, hoping to somehow stumble my way home. Robard, on reflection, may have been right. I assumed it would take weeks for someone to reach the northern coast if they *knew* where they were going. Traveling blind like this was a bad idea.

But I truly believed it was safer than trying to find a port city. Carry on, Tristan, I told myself. Beauseant!

It didn't work.

Maryam seethed with silent rage as we made our way through the woods. For no better reason than it was familiar to us, we followed the stream north again. Once past Celia's campsite from the night before, we would enter unknown territory.

After a while I tried again to engage Maryam in conversation, but despite my efforts she remained sullen. I knew her anger was not directed at me, but the farther we traveled, the more I wished to have the old Maryam back.

As we rounded a bend in the stream, the wind picked up and Angel suddenly stiffened, then growled. She had smelled something on the breeze, and sensing her alarm, Maryam and I stopped in our tracks.

Angel paced forward, standing rigid, her nose working the air.

"What do you think she smells?" Maryam asked quietly.

"Don't know. Most likely a squirrel," I answered. But I didn't believe it. Something in her manner urged caution. Silently I drew my short sword. I was about to encourage Maryam to draw her daggers, but a quick glance showed me they were already in her hands. How had she done that?

"Easy, girl," I said to Angel. "Let's go."

The three of us moved silently along the stream, the sound of our movements muffled by the bubbling water. Several yards past the campsite, Angel stopped to sniff at something on the ground.

"Maryam," I whispered. "Is that . . . ?"

"Yes," she answered.

A large spot of blood covered the leaves and ferns lining the forest floor. Something big had been killed or severely wounded nearby.

"Maybe we should take a different route," I offered.

Maryam shrugged. In her present state, with her pent-up anger at Robard, I thought she might actually enjoy finding something to fight.

Angel sauntered past the blood and this time kept her nose to the ground, moving quietly along the stream. Then without warning, she let out a bark and took flight, charging ahead. She bounded into the nearby underbrush and disappeared from sight.

"Dog . . . Angel!" I stammered. "Come back!"

We crept forward through the thicket until we reached Angel, barking and pawing at the ground near a large oak. As we approached her, I nearly screamed when a man fell from behind the tree and onto the ground.

I circled around to the front of the man while Maryam held her position at the rear. When I could see his face, I was shocked to discover I knew him.

It was Philippe.

His shirtfront was covered in blood. One of his arms looked broken, and as I knelt beside him, his eyes opened. He looked up at me and said, "Celia! *Vous devez la sauver!*"

Then he pitched forward and collapsed in my arms.

"What did he say?" Maryam asked.

"He said, 'Celia. You must save her.'"

hilippe was barely breathing. I knelt beside him and cut away his shirt with my small knife. A large wound just below his heart still bled. Having seen men die on the battlefield, I was amazed that Philippe was still alive and that he'd managed the strength to crawl as far as he had through the trees. I also realized there was nothing I could do for him.

"What should we do?" Maryam asked.

"There is nothing we can do except pray for his soul," I said.

"He was a fellow warrior," she said sadly, kneeling in the familiar position that I knew meant she was praying.

"Yes, he was," I replied quietly.

I studied Philippe again. His sword was missing. There was no sign of his horse.

"Who do you think could have done this?" Maryam asked. "Was it this High Counsel?"

"I don't know. Philippe was always circling back to see if they were being followed. It could be they . . ."

Philippe reached up and grabbed my arm, and I yelped in surprise. His eyes flew open, and with every bit of will he had, he focused on me. My heart pounded in my chest and my breath stopped.

"Templar! You must save her. I'm nearly done. The High Counsel will not rest until he crushes her and her father. Swear to me." So Philippe *could* speak English! I had been right after all.

"Philippe, what happened? How were you hurt?" I asked.

He struggled for breath.

"The High Counsel left a small force behind, trailing north. They must have found my tracks from my earlier scouts and guessed I would ride back to check. Six of them ambushed me." He coughed then, and a horrible gurgling sound came from his chest. He groaned in agony.

"Where are they now?"

"Four of them are dead," he said. He stopped, still struggling to breathe.

"Let me see if I can treat . . ."

"NO!" he said, and squeezed my arm so tightly that I thought the bones would break. Even near death his strength was remarkable. He groaned and closed his eyes, then raised his head again to speak.

"No. Leave now. Celia will move everyone from the villages to Montségur, our fortress, but the High Counsel will not give up easily. You are a soldier. You are needed there. Celia needs you. Jean-Luc, the others, they are far too young . . . and inexperienced . . . Good men, but they have never seen a real battle. Celia . . . she said she saw something in you. I was not . . ." He closed his eyes for a few seconds, but then his head came up again.

"I . . . was not . . . impressed," he said. He gripped my arm. "But you have returned here, so you must be braver than I thought. Now go. They will need your help. Go."

"Philippe, I will see you are given a Christian burial—" I started to say.

"No! No time. We are Cathars! We care not for the church and its rules. Leave my bones where they fall. Go. Swear to me you will go to her," he said. "Templars give an oath to protect the innocent, do they not?"

"Yes."

"Then as a soldier, promise you will defend her. On my soul, she and her people . . . our people . . . are innocent," he groaned, and closed his eyes again.

"You have my vow, Philippe. I will go to her," I said, placing my free hand over his. "Everything I can do, I will. On my honor as a Templar."

Philippe nodded. Angel whined again as Philippe took one more ragged breath and life left him. Maryam bowed her head and said a few more quiet words. For reasons I couldn't understand, I felt a profound sadness. Philippe had certainly not cared for me, but I offered up a silent prayer for this man who had so bravely given his life for his friends.

"Let's go," I said, starting back through the woods toward the stream. Maryam called behind me.

"Tristan, wait. What about Philippe? We can't just leave him here."

"You heard him. He made his wishes clear."

"Yes, but you can't just not bury the poor man," she said. Sir Thomas had once told me how the Saracens had very strict laws governing the handling and burial of their dead.

"Maryam, I know how you feel. But Philippe's faith was his own.

It is not our place to question him. He asked me to go to Celia's aid as quickly as possible. Burying him will take hours."

"Stop!" she shouted at me. I stopped.

"What do you think you're doing, Tristan? What is going on here?"

"I . . . You saw. Philippe is dead; Celia and her people need my help."

"Do they now?" I wasn't sure but I thought I detected just an edge of disgust or maybe sarcasm in Maryam's voice.

"Yes. You heard Philippe. They are in trouble. I promised I would try to help them."

"So you'll forget your 'vital' mission and traipse off to help someone you just met and hardly know?"

"Maryam, please. Philippe just gave his life for his people! They are obviously in grave danger. You heard me swear an oath to help. An *oath*, Maryam. We Templars tend to take such promises very seriously. I cannot—"

"Tristan, I don't believe you for a minute," she interrupted me. "You're using this oath as an excuse to go back to this girl."

"Well, you are entitled to your thoughts. But I assure you . . ."

Maryam held up a hand.

"What do you think you're doing, squire? Putting you—and me, for that matter—in danger? Before you met this girl, you were single-mindedly focused on getting to England with your 'dispatches.' Have you stopped to consider everything? What if you go to this place and find Celia? What if you don't make it out alive? What will happen to your mission then?"

"If you didn't want to come with me, maybe you should have

gone with Robard," I said. But I regretted it instantly, for I'd said it more harshly than I'd wished. Maryam didn't deserve such a sharp reply.

She didn't flinch from my words though.

"Maybe I should have. But I didn't. And I have my reasons. But nothing before this has dissuaded you from finding a way to England. Not Sir Hugh, not nearly drowning in a storm or being stranded in a strange country. But you meet this girl, you swear an 'oath' and all of a sudden your mission is forgotten. I think Robard was right. It's not *oath* at all. You *are* smitten."

"That's ridiculous," I said. "Are you questioning my honor?"

"Is it? Is it really ridiculous? You tell me."

Maryam's words made me wince, for in truth she was right on the mark. For reasons I could not explain, I had thought of little more than Celia since watching her and her group ride off. When we'd encountered the High Counsel on the beach, my first thought was of her safety. Though I barely knew her, I was suddenly consumed with finding her and making sure she was safe. Was this what being smitten meant? I had no idea. Before I'd left the monastery, I'd barely even seen a girl. And more important, *did* I make a promise to Philippe only because it gave me the chance to see her again?

"Maryam . . . she . . . I am not smitten," I said defensively.

"Yes, you are."

"I am not," I said.

"Are."

"I am . . . *Stop* it! She . . . I . . . am only . . . I have an obligation to her since she came to my aid when I was shipwrecked. Now I've promised Philippe whatever help I can give. There is a debt unpaid."

"Really? All I heard her do was ridicule you for joining the Knights Templar."

"She did not." All right. In truth, really, she had. But Maryam hadn't heard any of the nice things she'd said. Or seen her face in the moonlight. She hadn't witnessed the ice-blue pools of Celia's eyes. Oh dear.

"Hmph." Maryam sounded disgusted.

I tried to apologize. "Maryam, I'm sorry . . ."

She held up her hand again. I was becoming very familiar with the hand. At least it didn't have a dagger in it.

"Let's go," she said with disgust. She pushed past me and made her way back to the stream, turning north. She said nothing for a long while as I stumbled along behind her.

"How are we even going to find her?" she finally asked, her voice still dripping with anger.

A good question. A very good question.

And in truth I had absolutely no idea.

# In the Southern Pyrenees

e hiked along for several leagues. Before leaving the campsite, I'd found more wild grapes, so at least we had something to eat. With the sun high in the sky we paused to rest awhile. After catching our breath, we kept to the stream, and I kept careful watch for the spot where Celia and her followers had left its shallows. I was no forester, and truly missed Robard then, but studied the ground as closely as I could. Drawing on my memory of conversations with Celia and her group, I knew only that their base lay somewhere north. Without some kind of trail to follow I would most likely miss it completely.

A few leagues farther north, I found a spot where several horses had climbed the bank. The tracks kept to a trail through the woods, and so we followed. A few hours later, twilight approached, and the woods opened into a wide meadow. The countryside had gotten hilly, and from the clearing, I could see mountains far off in the distance. No one had said anything about mountains. I guess since *Mont* meant "mountain" in French, the name of her fortress, Montségur, should have warned me.

"We should rest here for the night," Maryam suggested, and I agreed. We had journeyed far and were weary. Angel ate a few grapes from my hand, then dropped immediately to the ground and was asleep instantly, her tongue lolling gently out of her mouth. I gave Maryam some grapes as well, and we found comfortable spots on the ground to sleep through the night.

The next day as we crossed the meadow, the tracks joined up with a dirt road that wound through the forest. The hoofprints of Celia's horses soon mixed with the signs of other travelers, including carts and wagons. After another hour of walking we entered a small village. It was little more than a wide spot along the trail, with a tiny chapel, an inn and a few other buildings lining the crossroads.

"Tristan, I don't know about you, but I'm starving," Maryam said. "Do you think we might be able to find something to eat here besides grapes?"

We stood off to the side of the trail and watched what few people there were in the village milling about. The church looked deserted, and we were too late in the day for morning mass. A small blacksmith shop was busy, and a few women gathered near a well across the path from the inn.

"Let's give it a try," I said, heading toward the inn.

Angel waited, curled up in a bed of grass a few steps off the trail. Maryam and I crossed through the center of the village and entered the front door. It was dark inside, with only one window at the front letting in any light, and smelled like wet dirt and wood smoke. A small fireplace with a sputtering flame took up one end of the room, and a doorway covered by a cloth curtain led away to the back. No one was in the main room, but we heard the sounds of activity beyond the curtained door.

*"Salut?"* I called out. Hello.

The curtain was pulled back and a woman of indeterminate age emerged. She wore a simple peasant frock of gray cloth, and a brown head scarf. She eyed us suspiciously, and for an instant a tremendous weight pressed down on me. I had a vision of Sir Hugh riding into the village and questioning this woman. She would tell him how we'd stopped here just a few short days ago and which direction we'd headed. But we needed food. There was no way around it.

This was never going to work. I was stuck here, and could speak enough French to get by, but Maryam and I could never pass as natives. As soon as I asked for food, she would know I was an outsider. Sir Hugh would be able to find us easily.

I spoke to the woman in the best French I could muster, silently cursing myself for not paying closer attention when Brother Rupert had sought to teach me his native tongue.

*"Aliments, s'il vous plaît?"* I asked, pointing to Maryam and myself.

She said nothing, moving to the fireplace where an iron pot hung on a hook over the coals. Using the front of her smock, she lifted the kettle off the hook and brought it to the table, motioning for us to sit. I peered into the kettle and saw some type of still-bubbling pottage.

The woman went through the curtain and returned seconds later with two wooden bowls and spoons, a small loaf of bread and an earthen jug. She sat it all on the table before us and made motions for us to fill the bowls and eat. So we did.

The pottage tasted far better than it looked. Maryam smiled and concentrated on eating. The woman reappeared with two cups and poured wine from the jug, and Maryam's eyes went wide.

"Tristan," she whispered. "I'm forbidden to drink wine."

"Give me a minute. I'll try to distract her somehow," I said.

The woman stood a few paces away, watching us. I lifted my mug and raised it in her direction.

"*Croisés!*" I said, letting her know we were Crusaders. Perhaps I could win us some points by appealing to the woman's sense of Christian duty. She smiled and nodded, then left for the back room again. I drank down a large gulp of wine and quickly poured what was in Maryam's cup into my own. A few seconds later the woman emerged with a small wheel of cheese, setting it on the table before us.

My mouth watered at the sight of it, and I took a proffered slice. I placed it on a slice of bread and bit into it. What a delight. After many days of nothing but dates, grapes and figs, and whatever we could scrounge up, it tasted wonderful.

A familiar barking sounded from just outside the door. I thought Angel might have smelled the food and was hungry herself. Wearily I rose to my feet and took a small chunk of cheese. I was about to open the door when she growled, and I froze. I then stepped to the dirty window and peered out at the crossroads.

The High Counsel and his fifty men rode into the village, reining their horses up at the well. Angel whined, and I cracked open the door. She darted inside.

"Trouble," I said to Maryam. She joined me at the window and gasped.

"What are we going to do?" she asked.

By then the woman had joined us at the window. She looked out at the High Counsel and his troop, some of whom had dismounted and were standing about looking menacing. The arrival had cleared the village, as the women we had seen earlier at the well had vanished and the blacksmith had made himself scarce.

The woman muttered something in French under her breath that I didn't quite catch but was fairly certain was a curse. She vanished behind the curtain.

"It looks like the High Counsel has uncovered my deception. They must be headed toward Celia's fortress. We need to get out of here. I don't suppose you have any ideas, do you?" I asked.

Maryam shook her head and continued to study the scene at the well. "No. You're the one with the *ideas*," she said smugly.

Angel whined nervously, and to quiet her I tossed her the small chunk of cheese I still held in my hand. She snatched it out of the air and swallowed it whole.

"All right," I said. "Maybe we can sneak out the back and . . ."

Just then the woman pulled back the curtain from the back room and waved to us.

We followed and found another room, nearly equal in size to the one we'd been eating in but with a back entrance. The wooden door swung open, and there stood a boy about ten or twelve years old, waiting next to a small wagon with a pony hitched to it. The back of the wagon was full of hay.

"Hide. Go," said the woman in accented English.

"Tristan? What is she . . . ?" Maryam asked, but she stopped, not understanding completely what was happening.

But I did. Or at least I thought I did. Since we had left the campsite, without really knowing how far we needed to travel to reach Celia, I'd had a feeling we were at least getting close to her lands. And judging by this woman's reaction when she saw the High Counsel, I decided to test my assumption.

"Cathar?" I said to the woman.

She nodded and smiled. She pushed a small cloth bag into my hands, holding it open. It was full of bread, cheese and apples.

"Montségur. Celia. *Ami,*" I said, pointing to myself.

The woman nodded and smiled. I felt a brief sense of relief, despite the High Counsel's arrival. We were on the right trail and headed toward Montségur.

"Hide. Now," she said.

"Come on, Maryam," I said.

I climbed up into the bed of the wagon. Maryam joined me. Angel looked at me with her head cocked.

"Hurry, girl," I said.

She jumped up. The boy and the woman covered us with the hay. Then I heard the lad whistle and the wagon moved. We rolled around the side of the small inn and bounced over the bumpy ground. The ride smoothed out a little when we reached the trail leading out of town.

I carefully reached up and cleared a small section of hay out of the way so I could see the village crossroads as we left. The High Counsel stood there, still talking to one of his soldiers in the street. The boy kept a casual pace with the wagon, not drawing attention to himself. He was just a simple farm boy completing one of his many chores.

We were almost out of sight of the village when I heard a cracking sound and the wagon lurched to a stop. It tilted crazily to the side, and Maryam and I grunted sharply as it hit the ground. The boy muttered a curse, and I assumed the wagon's axle had broken or the wheel had come loose. Angel whimpered, and I grabbed her about the muzzle. The hay had settled with the fall, and I gently cleared another space to look back at the village.

As I watched them in the distance, nearly two hundred yards away, the High Counsel and his men mounted up, steered their horses about and rode down the path.

They were headed straight for us.

he High Counsel took the head of the column and spurred his horse along the trail. The jangling sounds of swords and chain mail grew louder as the riders drew near. Then, softly, a familiar humming filled the air around me. Having heard it so many times before, I was relieved at first, but I still worried. I felt the Grail would protect me. But what about Maryam and the boy? What if the boy were forced to reveal our presence?

He wasn't visible from my position in the hay, but I offered up a prayer that he had the good sense to remain calm and not draw attention to himself. My hand was still firmly clamped over Angel's muzzle and she wiggled beneath my grasp. We held our breath for what seemed an eternity.

As the horses thundered toward us, she became more anxious and struggled so much that I lost my grip on her. She wormed her way out of the pile of hay and jumped off the back of the wagon, barking madly at the horses. I couldn't see anything, but outside the wagon she put up quite a fuss. Even worse, the column reined to a stop.

Angel ceased barking, but continued to growl and whine.

Maryam and I lay frozen beneath the mound of hay, and the beating of my own heart pounded in my ears, nearly drowning out the whispering hum of the Grail.

The High Counsel spoke to the boy in a gruff, commanding voice, but his words were muffled by the hay, as was the boy's reply.

Then there was only silence. Every muscle in my body was coiled and tense as if I'd been frozen solid in a sudden winter storm. The only sounds reaching my ears were Angel's whine and the snorts of the horses as they waited impatiently to resume their trip.

The High Counsel spoke again, but I could only hear the boy answer, *"Oui."* Angel quieted. We waited and waited, and I half expected a sword or lance to come poking into the hay.

Finally he gave an order to move out. The horses sprang to life and we heard them ride off.

Dizzy and light-headed, I took slow, deep breaths while the feeling returned to my limbs. Angel jumped back up onto the wagon and dug at the hay in an attempt to uncover us. The boy knocked twice on the side of the wagon.

*"La voie est libre,"* he told us. All clear.

We sat up, pushing the hay out of the way. I jumped out of the wagon and vigorously shook the boy's hand several times.

"Well done, *mon ami*. Well done," I said. I wanted to thank him more profusely but wasn't sure my French was adequate for the task.

Maryam, whose clothing and hair was covered in bits of hay, thanked him as well.

He smiled, and the expression on his face said he was more than happy to help two slightly crazed, hay-encrusted strangers.

I examined the wagon with the boy, and we discovered that the wheel on one side had indeed slipped off the axle. I offered to help him repair it, but he would have none of it. He waved us on our way.

He pointed to the trail we stood on, then lifted his arm and pointed up toward the mountains in the distance. "Montségur."

His meaning was clear.

I bowed to the boy in gratitude. It was unusual to see such courage and cool-headedness in a boy so young, and for a moment, though he looked nothing like him, his manner and disposition reminded me of Quincy, my friend and fellow squire whom I had left behind in Acre. His memory came rushing back to me, and I was overcome by feelings of regret.

"Very well. *Merci*," I said. Maryam was busy pulling bits of hay from her hair, but she waved good-bye to the boy. Gathering up the small bag of food, we took to the road. Angel fell into step a few paces in front of us.

"Next time, Little D— . . . Angel," I said, "try to stay quiet when enemy soldiers are about."

She kept trotting ahead of us, ignoring my admonition, and bounded about, rushing to and fro as if madness had overcome her.

"Angel, you need to be quiet. Stop acting foolish. There could still be . . ."

"Tristan?" Maryam interrupted.

"Yes?"

"You do realize you're talking to a dog?"

"Yes."

"She can't understand you. You didn't by chance hit your head on the hay wagon, did you?" she said with mock concern.

"She heard me. She just chooses to ignore me."

Maryam's ill temper had returned, and we walked on in silence awhile longer. Several times, I found myself slowing my pace, as she appeared to have no interest in moving quickly along the trail. Fearing she would tear my head off if I asked her to hurry, I remained quiet.

"What do you suppose has become of Robard?" she finally asked. At last, I thought. She wants to talk about it.

"I don't know. He must have reached Perpignan by now. I hope he found a ship," I said gently.

"I wish he hadn't left," she said with a catch in her voice.

"I know."

I looked at Maryam and thought I saw tears in her eyes. She looked away.

"Maryam?" I asked a while later when she had composed herself.

"Yes?"

"Can you explain something to me? A question about men and women? Keeping in mind I grew up in a monastery?"

She laughed. "I'll try."

"You're sad Robard is gone," I said.

"I am."

"Yet when we were together, you argued constantly. Quite heatedly, I might add. But when he tried to leave, you did everything you could to talk him out . . ."

Maryam chuckled again. "I know. He can be incredibly annoying. But often, as you've seen, he is brave and noble. After we lost you in the ocean, we were still tied to the deck of the ship. The storm worsened and I was certain we were going to die. Robard kept telling me to hang on, he wasn't going to let anything happen to me.

When the ship broke apart, we went under, but Robard managed to get both me and Angel to the surface. He grabbed on to a piece of wreckage and we held on to it together. All the time he kept talking calmly to us, over the roaring wind and thrashing waves. He repeatedly told me we would be fine. We just needed to make it through the storm. Several times I thought I would lose my grip and sink into the water, but Robard wouldn't allow it."

Maryam gazed off into the distance as she walked. She had a smile on her face as she remembered, which I thought odd, because I would have done anything to forget such a terrifying experience. Then I realized she wasn't remembering almost drowning. She was remembering Robard saving her.

"I lost consciousness a few times, but Robard held on to both of us. The next thing I remember is waking up on the shore with a fire going and Angel licking my face. Robard must have carried both of us out of the water, because I have no recollection of getting there. When I asked him what had happened, he just shrugged and changed the subject."

Her story gave me pause, and I wondered if the Grail, even though I carried it with me, had extended its protection to my friends. The fact of their survival was miraculous to me. Was it another miracle of this sacred relic, or did Robard save them by himself?

"There's no question of Robard's bravery," I said. "And he is a decent fellow. He has just grown weary of the war and misses his home and family. It's hard to blame him for wishing to return there as quickly as possible."

"I suppose," she answered. I still didn't understand though. The brothers had explained the ways of men and women to me, and had told me that someday I might wish to marry when I left St. Alban's. Yet, so far, I found women . . . puzzling.

As we walked, the path got steeper and the mountains we had first observed from far off drew nearer. It grew colder as we climbed higher. The trail we followed was well traveled, marked with numerous ruts made by wagon wheels and horse tracks. The boy had said we could follow this trail all the way to Montségur, but had given no indication of how far it was.

The sun rose high in the sky and we kept on northward. Each time we came to a village or town, we either went around it and found the trail again, or moved through it as quickly as we could, trying hard to remain invisible. After a few more hours of walking, we stopped in a shaded glen to eat. Angel ate her fill of cheese and apples and curled up next to me for a nap. For a brief instant, sitting there in the beautiful spot, I forgot everything: the Grail, my duty, and the fact that Robard had left us. I even forgot about Sir Hugh, and the High Counsel and his men, who were undoubtedly trying to find me.

I sat beneath the shade of the trees and watched the sunlight filter its way through the leaves and dance across the ground. It was refreshing. The soreness that plagued me from my adventure in the ocean left me. It was amazing what rest and food could do to restore one's spirits. But the feeling was fleeting.

I wished to stay longer, but we had to press on. After an hour we rose to our feet and resumed our march north. We talked some, but finally concentrated on making good time. Back in Outremer, we had at one point run nearly nonstop for several days to make our way to Tyre in advance of the attacking Saracens. The High Counsel had a head start, and I suppose we could have quickened our pace.

But Celia knew the High Counsel was coming, and as long as he didn't catch her before she reached the fortress, she should be safe. I would be no good to her if I arrived exhausted. I would need my wits and energy about me.

We walked on and on, finally silent, as we had grown too tired to talk anymore. The sun was sinking in the west, and we would need to find a place to bed down for the night soon. It had been a very long day.

But thoughts of rest vanished when an anguished scream pierced the air.

# 12

hat was that?" Maryam asked, her daggers ready as she scanned the trail ahead of us.

"I don't know. It sounded like a woman's scream," I said. "It came from up ahead." Angel paced cautiously ahead of us. She sniffed and tossed her head, and we crept quietly along.

A few yards farther up the trail, we approached the outskirts of a settlement. Another scream startled us both, and we leapt off the trail into the safety of the trees. Maryam crouched, petting the dog to keep her calm. I drew my short sword and peered through the trees at the buildings ahead, trying to get a sense of what was happening.

It was a small village, like the one we'd stopped at a few hours before, with about a dozen wooden dwellings and a few other buildings crowded alongside the trail. It looked deserted. Then there was a louder and even more tormented scream that echoed off the trees around us.

Angel looked up at me with her brown, intelligent eyes. I held my fingers to my lips and told her to stay. She stared back at me and whined quietly, then lay down on the ground, her small tail bobbing madly back and forth.

I gestured for Maryam to follow me.

We crept up behind the first small dwelling. With my back to the wall, I peered around the corner toward the interior of the village but saw nothing. The only sound was the breeze as it moved through the woods. Then I thought I heard a muffled cry coming from a small cluster of buildings a few yards ahead. I motioned for Maryam to go around the other side and work her way forward. She melted away in an instant, and I carefully stepped around the corner, my sword at the ready.

The doorway of the hut was open, but with a quick look inside I found it deserted. I moved quickly past it and on to the next building. Also empty. There was a murmur of voices up ahead, mingled with the sounds of soft cries. Still advancing forward, and pausing at the space between two of the huts, I found Maryam waiting for me. She had heard the noise as well, and signaled for us to keep moving toward it as she faded away again.

A few paces ahead I came to the last building facing the village square. I peered cautiously around the corner to find two of the High Counsel's men standing, swords drawn, before a man slumped to the ground with his hands tied behind his back. A young boy and girl were sobbing uncontrollably, clutching their mother's skirts a few steps away.

Looking down the side of the building, Maryam was already studying the scene from her vantage point. Her eyes found mine and I nodded for her to meet me out of sight of the two men.

"What is the meaning of this?" she whispered, her voice quivering with anger.

"I don't know. What do you suppose this man has done to be tied up so?"

Maryam shrugged. "Maybe they are some of Celia's people. If they couldn't make it to the fortress, perhaps they hid out here and were discovered by those cretins."

"I wonder if those are the two men who survived the encounter with Philippe," I pondered.

"Safe to assume. They must be on their way to Montségur to rejoin their forces. What are we going to do?"

"I don't know yet." I tried to concentrate, but then from the other side of the hut came a loud smack and another scream. I didn't know what was happening, but I had little patience for those who would injure innocent people.

"Circle through the woods and work your way to the far side of the buildings. I'll draw their attention and try to get them to chase me. When they do, take those people to the woods and find a place to hide."

Maryam nodded and left me there. I counted to one hundred very slowly to give her time to move into position. Then I stepped out where the men would see me.

One of the soldiers was holding the bound man's hair in his clenched fist while the other tried to work a length of rope around his neck. The boy launched himself at the two men, his small arms flailing and kicking at the villain who held his father's hair. The man laughed and backhanded the lad, sending him sprawling in the dirt.

That did it.

"What is the meaning of this?" I shouted.

Both men were so startled that they jumped, releasing their grip on the father, who slowly keeled over in the dirt. They looked at me and drew their swords.

*"Qui êtes-vous?"* the one closest to me shouted. I was fairly certain he was asking me who I was. Curse my poor French!

"What are you doing to these people?" I asked in English. Both men stared at me in confusion.

The first man spoke quickly, and it was hard for me to follow. But from what I could understand, they were going to execute the man.

I had no idea what else to say or how to communicate with them. So I ordered them to let the man and family go free. "Leave these people alone," I commanded.

He spoke rapidly again. I couldn't understand everything, but I heard the word *Cathar* and he pointed to the family. They must be some of Celia's people.

"I demand you release him," I said, trying to put as much menace in my voice as I could.

The two men looked at each other, then back at me, and burst out laughing.

*"Non,"* they said. They must have understood some of what I'd said. Or like Celia and her party, they *did* speak English, but chose not to reveal it. Was everyone in this cursed country so deceitful when it came to language?

"In the name of the Knights Templar I demand you step aside," I said, rising up slightly on the balls of my feet, ready to move.

They did not answer but started for me. I retreated slowly, trying to draw them away from the family. Maryam emerged from between two buildings on the other side of the square, and silently moved toward the family.

When I had drawn the men past the first hut, I stopped and let them close in on me, all the while keeping Maryam in my peripheral vision. She had reached the people now, and with her dagger, quickly cut the man's bonds and tried to rouse him. She needed more time.

The men had smiles on their faces as they approached. They had the advantage in numbers, skill and experience. I had only my sword and my righteous indignation.

"Tell me," I said. "Do you enjoy beating up small children?"

The men just kept coming forward, but they were cautious now. They saw the short blade in my hand and Sir Thomas' weapon laced across my back and would not be easily duped. Maryam had managed to pull the woman to her feet, and together they were lifting up the husband. She carried the unconscious boy under one arm, and the little girl followed along as they headed toward the woods.

And then my plan fell apart.

The soldier closest to me caught me looking behind him and looked back to find Maryam leading the family away. He cursed and his companion immediately took off toward them.

"Maryam! Look out!" I shouted.

She looked back to see the soldier closing fast.

Maryam handed the boy to the mother, pushed her and the girl toward the woods and lowered the unconscious father to the ground. As the soldier approached, she ululated in her horrible Hashshashin war cry and drew her daggers, waiting for his charge as he came at her, sword high.

The other soldier raised his sword and charged me. I quickly darted between the buildings and raced around the far corner, with him fast behind me. I wanted him to chase me, for I was afraid if I stood and fought, he could easily defeat me before the woman and her children could hide. I ran quickly around the building and tried to circle back on him. I'd temporarily lost sight of him and paused at the next corner, my back to the wall, trying to hear over Maryam's shouts.

I waited. Five seconds. Ten. Then a shadow fell across the ground, coming slowly toward the corner. When it was close enough, I jumped out, swinging with all my might.

But he was expecting it and ducked my swing. My blade glanced off the timber of the hut. He thrust back at me, and I barely pulled my sword back in time to block his stroke.

We traded blow upon blow, both of us swinging desperately. He tried to push me back against the wall of the hut, but I refused to give ground. Then he swung at me with an overhead strike, and as I raised my sword up to block his blade, he slashed me across the forearm. I gasped in pain, and staggered backward. He raised his weapon again and came at me. I launched myself at him before he could bring the blade down and hit him squarely in the chest with my shoulder. He stumbled backward, giving me time to switch hands.

My arm burned and I was angry now. I tried to remain cool, but images of Philippe and the small boy being treated like an animal clouded my vision. Swinging wildly, I gave him no chance to mount an offensive, but he was calm and parried each attack.

Rage was not gaining me anything; he was too good. I needed a deception, trickery of some sort. I also had to stop the bleeding in my arm. Where was the power of the Grail when I needed it? It remained silent, nestled in the bottom of the satchel hanging across my back.

I moved out from the wall to my right, keeping him at bay with my sword. Then I stepped in as close as I could get to the corner of the hut. I took a wild swing at him to draw him in, and as I hoped, he reared back to bring his sword around in a mighty arc. Instead of blocking it this time, I ducked and the blade whistled over my head. When the sword hit the corner of the hut, it bit into the soft timber and was stuck there. His eyes went wide as he yanked desperately to free his blade. Not giving him the chance, I ducked under his arm and rose up, driving the hilt of my sword as hard as I could into the side of his head. It connected with a solid thump and the man's eyes rolled up in his head. He slumped to the ground unconscious.

Breathing hard, I worked his sword free from the side of the hut and tossed it as far as I could into the woods. I searched him quickly, removed a dagger from his belt and threw it away as well.

Racing back to where I'd last seen Maryam, I came around the side of the building and found her sprawled on the ground. She had lost her daggers and rolled over, crawling on her hands and knees, desperately trying to reach them. The soldier closed in on her, his sword raised. She was helpless and about to die unless I could reach her in time.

But I didn't have to, for an arrow suddenly appeared in the center of the soldier's chest. He looked down in shock at the instrument of his death, and then tumbled backward to the dirt.

I spun around to see Robard standing there. Maryam looked up from the ground in wonder.

"Robard?" she said, her face breaking into a wide smile.

"Hello, Assassin," he said, grinning. "Did you miss me?"

# 13

y mouth hung open as if I'd been struck dumb. He smiled and gave us a jaunty little salute. A black-clad blur rushed past me, and Maryam took Robard in a fierce embrace. Momentarily startled by the force of her attention, he held his arms out gingerly to the side while she wrapped hers around his back.

"You came back," she said, unable to keep the joy from her voice.

"I did. Um. Maryam?" he said.

"Yes," she said, looking up at him but still not releasing her hold.

"I can't breathe," he said.

She laughed and buried her head in his chest, hugging him tighter.

"Assassin?" he coughed. "I'm serious. Can't breathe."

She let go of him then and stepped back, her face aglow. "You're really here. You came back," she said.

"Yes, I came back. The two of you wouldn't likely make your way back to England without me."

"Couldn't find a ship in Perpignan?" I asked.

"Not a one!" He laughed. "No. In truth, I followed the High Counsel and his troops toward Perpignan and had the chance to see some of their work up close. The afternoon after they left us on the beach, they burned a village to the ground. Dragged all the people out of their homes and shops and torched it completely. Even their church. I could only watch from the woods. I don't know what he said to those people, but I've heard men like him before. He enjoyed terrifying them. He delighted in burning them out of their homes."

I nodded, understanding exactly what he was saying.

Robard shrugged.

"When they didn't find Celia in Perpignan, they headed back this way. I knew you had headed in the same direction and decided if you were going to tangle with this High Counsel fellow, you were going to need some help."

I smiled. Robard had a conscience after all. His bravery had never been in doubt, but I was deeply touched by his compassion.

Maryam still stared at Robard, gripping his arms. Robard smiled at her.

"Maryam?" he asked.

"Hmm. Yes?" she replied.

"May I have my arms back?"

She finally released him. "You came back," she said, as if she had just woken from a dream.

"Yes, I did. Now we have work," he said gently.

As happy as we were to see Robard, Angel was happiest of all. She burst out of the woods where she had been guarding the mother and the two children and raced to Robard's side, jumping and barking happily at him. He laughed and scooped her up in his arms.

"I guess I just couldn't leave you behind, girl," he joked. He put her down and she raced around us madly, turning back and forth and barking.

The woman and her children emerged from the woods and rushed to the side of the father, who still lay where Maryam had left him.

"Maryam, maybe you should assist them while Robard and I attend to these soldiers," I said quietly.

She nodded and with a last glance at Robard, trotted to the side of the woman. Angel loped after Maryam, and Robard stared after them.

"What happened to the big Frenchman I had the fight with?" he asked.

"Philippe! You found him?"

"Yes."

"He encountered a squad of the High Counsel's men. There was a fight and he killed four of them, but he died from his wounds."

"Killed four? By himself?" Robard said, incredulous.

I nodded.

"Tough man, that Frank," he added, impressed.

"Yes, he was."

"I guess it's lucky I got here in time to be of use."

"Yes. But how did you find us?"

"You were easy enough to follow. Your boots leave a distinctive track. And I knew you were headed north. So I just followed the main trail. Don't forget, I lived my whole life in a forest. I know how to track people."

"Have you seen anyone else about? Any of the High Counsel's men? Any Templar regimentos?"

"No. Since I left the spot where you camped last night, I've seen no one."

"We don't have much time to waste. Can you help me hide these men in the woods? I don't want them to be easily discovered if the High Counsel sends someone looking for them."

Robard nodded and we walked to the spot where I had left the man between the buildings.

Only he was no longer there. Robard pulled another arrow from his wallet and nocked it immediately. We peered around the corner of the hut, but the man was nowhere to be found.

"This is not good," I muttered.

"No, it's not," Robard agreed. "We need to get moving. If he has friends nearby . . ."

We quickly trotted to the center of the village.

The man who had been beaten by the two soldiers was coming around. Maryam held a water skin to his lips and his wife dabbed at the cuts on his face with a damp cloth. The young girl and boy stood off to the side, the boy holding his small hand to his face where an ugly purplish bruise was forming around his eye. My breath caught as I thought of the little one's brave attempt to defend his father.

"Is he going to be all right?" Robard asked.

"I think he'll survive. He has some broken ribs, but those are the worst of his injuries," Maryam said. She looked up at my bleeding arm and with her dagger cut a small piece of cloth from the hem of my tunic. Covering the wound, which was not serious, she tied it tightly.

"Thank you," I murmured.

Robard stepped to the dead soldier and inspected his handi-work. With his small knife, he cut the coin pouch from the soldier's belt.

He knelt beside the woman, who still held her husband, and offered it to her.

*"Madame, s'il vous plaît?"* he said, motioning for her to take the purse.

She looked confused and afraid. Robard lifted up her hand and placed the coins in it, closing his hand over it. He kept his hand there, nodding and smiling until the woman understood.

*"Merci,"* she said. *"Merci."* Then she started crying, which made Robard very uncomfortable. He stood up quickly and busied him-self inspecting the body of the fallen soldier. With little effort, he lifted the man up and threw him over his shoulder. I had forgotten how strong he was.

"Robard, what—" Maryam stammered, but he interrupted her.

"The High Counsel is rich. She is very poor, from the looks of it. This soldier clearly has no further use for the money. I fought for my king and country. For my father. But I despise men like this High Counsel. If I could, I would take every crosslet he had, every shilling, every bit of gold, and I would find the poorest peo-ple around and make him watch while they danced away with his wealth." Robard's face was filled with raw emotion. I had heard him say many similar things in Outremer as we walked along in the night. Now I had witnessed his principles up close, and it made me smile. Maryam was not the only one glad to have him back.

"Shall we?" he asked, nodding toward the north.

He started down the trail, carrying the dead man over his shoulder. Maryam and I followed behind and Angel raced ahead of us, running back and forth along the trail. When we were well out of the settlement, Robard disappeared in the woods and returned moments later without the dead soldier.

We walked on in silence, but there was a noticeable change in Maryam's demeanor. Her step was lighter and she floated along the trail. Robard didn't see it, as he was intent on getting to where we were going.

The trail took us higher and higher, and at last we cleared the woods along the rim of a long valley. And across the valley on a mountaintop sat a small fortress at the very tip of a high peak. It had to be the place.

Montségur.

# Montségur
## Late October 1191

※

# 14

wanted to push on, but Robard convinced me we should stop and rest for the night. The minute he suggested it I felt exhaustion overtake me and we found another copse of trees and bedded down for the night. We were up at first light and as we crossed the valley floor, we saw further evidence that the High Counsel and his men had been visiting. Several dwellings were destroyed, livestock had been killed, and the area was devoid of people. Celia had said Cathars often fled to the fortress when they were besieged, and I hoped they had found safety behind Montségur's walls before the High Counsel arrived.

"So, Templar, how do you plan on getting inside the castle?" Robard asked.

"I was just thinking the same thing!" Maryam blurted, smiling at him. Ever since he had rejoined us, she rarely took her eyes off him.

We had finally reached the base of the mountain after several hours of hiking over rough terrain. The fortress sat atop a tooth-shaped peak, and although the bottom was covered by trees, the summit was barren of most vegetation. It was rocky and lined with boulders and would be a difficult climb, even without the High Counsel and his men in the way.

From our vantage point, there was only one passable trail to the top, which is probably what made it such a strategic spot for a fortress. It would take an army of any size hours, if not days, to move into position to even launch an assault. It was amazing how a structure of its size could ever be built in such a place.

"Tristan?" Robard asked.

"Huh?" I replied, drawing my attention away from my study of the castle.

"The fortress? Any idea how we'll get inside?"

"None spring immediately to mind," I tried, but I failed to keep the resignation out of my voice.

"If Celia is inside there, she's probably safe. We can always just go around and keep moving north toward home," Robard said.

I shook my head.

"Oh no, we can't," Maryam said with more than a trace of disgust in her voice. "He made a promise to the Frenchman."

"Which Frenchman?" Robard asked.

"Philippe. The dead one." She smirked.

"What? A promise? What kind of promise?" Robard asked. I thought he would be angry, but he looked at me with curiosity.

"Keep in mind . . . he was dying. I may have . . . possibly sworn an oath to him I would help her, is all," I stammered.

"Help her how?" Robard asked.

"With her troubles with this High Counsel fellow," I said.

"What? Are you out of your mind? Did you not see the heavily armed men he rode with? You intend to help Celia and her merry band of peasants stand against that?" *Now* he was angry.

"Yes . . . I guess," I said. "It was an oath!"

Robard let out an exasperated sigh. "You *are* smitten with this girl!"

"What? No . . . of course not. I don't . . . she . . . I barely know her!" I said, embarrassed.

"That's right!" Maryam piped up. "He only just met her, when she tried to stab him!"

"She didn't try to stab . . . Oh, for heaven's sake." Maryam and Robard were smiling at each other while I squirmed in discomfort. So I stormed off through the woods and found a spot where the trees cleared a little and I had a better view of the mountaintop. Smitten, indeed. What rubbish. And besides, I'd seen the way Maryam and Robard had been looking at each other since his return. They were ones to make sport of me!

I simmered in my embarrassment for a while, studying the fortress and the grounds around it, trying to focus my mind on the problem at hand. I was certain Celia was inside. However, I had no idea how to get us inside or even how to get word to her.

A few minutes later Robard joined me, and he studied the terrain surrounding Montségur.

"I find it hard to believe they can have enough men and supplies to survive a long siege," he said.

"True enough. But the High Counsel rode with just fifty men. We also know Philippe narrowed their numbers by four and we took care of one more. Forty-odd men against those walls doesn't sound like much either. Celia said most of the time they hole up inside waiting until their attackers grow tired and leave."

"Hmm. Do you intend to wait here until that happens? It could

91

take days. Even weeks. By all we've seen, the High Counsel is a very determined fellow," he said.

"No. The longer we wait, the more time Sir Hugh has to catch up. I would prefer to get inside and help Celia drive off this villain, so I know she's safe and we can be on our way." I put my hand on the satchel. "I need to complete my mission. But I did give a dying man my promise."

Robard nodded.

"So we need a way in," he repeated.

"Yes."

Just then, a small squad of about twelve riders broke from the tree line near the summit and galloped toward the castle gate. We recognized the High Counsel's men immediately. From this distance it was impossible to tell if anyone manned the battlements of the castle, but the riders took no fire from the walls. They looked to be talking with someone inside. A short while later they turned their mounts and retreated from sight into the trees.

"So his eminence is definitely here," observed Robard.

I sat down on a fallen log, tired and dejected. The situation was impossible. What good was it to endure so much to reach Celia, when she was now further away than ever?

Robard sat next to me while Maryam lounged a few yards away. Angel had curled up in her lap and fallen fast asleep. There appeared to be no way for us to sneak into the castle, something like a hidden passage or some other minor miracle. I even toyed with the idea of making a run for the castle gate across the open ground. If we were seen, the High Counsel's men would ride us down long before we reached safety. There had to be a better plan, a way to get word to Celia we were here and to open the gate when the time was right, just long enough for the three of us to slip in ahead of the High Counsel and his men.

The barest flicker of an idea took hold.

"Robard, were we to get close enough, could you shoot an arrow over the walls and into the bailey?" I asked.

Robard looked up at Montségur again and studied it before answering.

"Of course, if it's only distance you're concerned with and not accuracy. However, I've a notion there'll be swirling winds atop the mountain, which could sway the shaft," he said.

"But you could do it?"

"I think so."

"Good. Then the only thing we need now is to relieve three of the High Counsel's men from their horses," I said.

"What?" Robard asked. Maryam moved Angel off her lap.

"Did I just hear you correctly?" she asked. "Horses? Are you mad?"

"No, but I am running out of time and options," I argued.

I filled them in on my plan.

"This might be the worst plan in the entire history of plans," Robard announced upon hearing my explanation.

"Agreed!" said Maryam.

"All right," I said. "If it's such a bad idea and you don't wish to participate, I understand."

I left them there and moved forward through the trees. Angel growled.

Robard shushed her. "Tristan, wait," he pleaded.

"No time to wait. I need to help Celia get rid of the High Counsel like I promised, and then we need to get moving before Sir

Hugh sends every remaining Templar regimento in the Kingdom of France after us. So unless the two of you have a better idea, we have no time to waste."

I kept walking forward and could hear some whispered conversation between them, but shortly they followed behind me.

"So how are we going to do this?" Robard asked.

"Do what? You mean execute the worst plan in the history of plans?" I said.

"Yes. The very one."

"First we need to get a message to Celia. I thought about trying to write her a note and attaching it to the arrow, but I have no quill. Besides, if I were in her position, I might think such a note from me is a trick. She may think the High Counsel followed us, captured me and is torturing me so he can deceive her."

We kept climbing ever upward toward the mountaintop, now moving more carefully in case the High Counsel had pickets posted in the area. We needed to remain silent, but now and then Robard and Maryam took the opportunity to whisper numerous reasons why my plan was full of holes. As if I didn't know it already. I ignored them and concentrated on getting us within an arrow's distance of the fortress without being seen. Caution slowed us down, and the steep incline of the mountain made it even more difficult.

After about an hour of deliberate movement, we reached a spot where the tree line faded and the ground cleared to rock. We looked about for any sign of the High Counsel and his men but saw none. Surely they had the castle under watch, but my guess was they stayed to the woods to keep out of the wind and remaining light.

I took a closer look at the castle. There was a large wooden gate facing southwest. It was the only way in. On the one hand, we were lucky there was no moat or drawbridge to cross. On the other hand, I was concerned my plan may not work at all. For Robard to send an arrow into the castle from here would require a miraculous shot. He would not only have to factor in the distance of at least three hundred yards, but he would also have to shoot up at an odd angle. It looked unlikely, if not impossible.

"It's not going to work," Maryam said. "If we leave the safety of the trees, we'll be spotted for sure. And there's no way Robard can make the shot from here. We're going to have . . ."

"What makes you think I can't make the shot, Assassin?" Robard cut in.

Maryam winked at me.

"Robard, I know you have great skill as an archer, but look at the angle. It's not your fault. It is just impossible. There is nothing to be ashamed of."

"Robard, Maryam might be right," I said.

"What? You too?" Robard looked at us both. "I could make this shot in my sleep. In fact, Assassin, I'll make a friendly wager. I make the shot and you hand over one of those fancy daggers of yours. If I miss, you can keep my longbow."

I gasped. Maryam was trying to goad Robard into doing what I wanted him to do, but as always, Robard took things a step too far. I had no wish for his foolish pride to get in the way.

"Robard . . . really, it's not necessary. I'll think of some other—" I stumbled over the words.

"Done," said Maryam.

I looked at her with eyes wide.

"No. Absolutely not. Maryam, I won't let you sacrifice your most prized possessions. And Robard, you told me your bow belonged to your father! Both of you stop this foolishness," I demanded.

"It did belong to my father. And his father before him. But I don't intend to miss."

"I've always wanted my own bow," Maryam said mischievously.

Robard pulled an arrow from the wallet at his back. He looked at it, sighting along its length to make sure it was straight and true.

"Tristan, what do you think, will she recognize my arrow?" he asked. I shrugged and stared up at the castle again, thinking hard. What would Celia think? If I sent her some type of message, would she know it was from me? Or would she expect a trick? Then I decided. If we could get close enough to the walls without being captured by the High Counsel, maybe she would be able to hear or recognize us. It was not a perfect plan, but it would have to do. The rest depended on Robard.

With a sigh, I removed Sir Thomas' Templar ring from my satchel. Robard nodded, and slid the ring over the point of the arrow along the shaft until it reached the feathers. I found a loose black thread on the edge of Maryam's tunic and pulled it from the cloth, and with it Robard wrapped the ring tightly to the arrow. He tested the weight and balance of the arrow in his hand until he was satisfied.

"I'm going to move out of the trees. I want to get a feel for the wind. Let's just hope no one spots me."

Robard trotted forward, bent at the waist. Within a few yards he had cleared the forest. He moved stealthily along, keeping his eyes on the fortress. There were no shouts of warning from the woods or calls of alarm. So far, so good.

A Templar ring, an English arrow and a thread from an Assassin's tunic. I offered up a silent prayer, begging God to guide the arrow. For good measure, I rubbed the satchel on the spot where the Grail lay in its secret compartment. I strained to hear the humming sound I'd heard before whenever I needed a miracle. If ever I needed one, it was now. But the Grail remained silent.

First, Robard needed to make the shot. Then someone needed to find the arrow and take it to Celia. Then she would need to discern its meaning. I had to trust she would know what to do when the time was right. That was the plan. Flimsy, with a great deal of luck needed for it to even have the remotest chance of working. But it was all I had.

Robard found a spot that suited him and squatted behind a large boulder, still intently studying the fortress above. He reached down and grasped a small handful of dirt, tossing it in the air, watching to see how the breeze moved it.

He waited, thirty yards away from us, and I silently bade him to hurry. We could be seen at any time. Finally, he stood and tested the pull of the bow a few times. Then he took his stance, feet slightly more than shoulder width apart, left arm straight and still, with the guard of the bow clutched firmly in his left hand. His right hand held the nock of the arrow gently between his fingers, and then he pulled back and I heard the familiar creak of wood and sinew.

"Maryam, no offense, but I hope you lose your bet," I murmured to her quietly.

And we watched in silent wonder as the arrow moved upward toward the heavens, flying at first as if it would not stop until it hit the sun. Then it arched over ever so gently and began its return to earth. I worried the arrow might hit someone inside the fortress and hurt, or even kill them. But then I thought the odds of a single random arrow finding flesh inside a mountain fortress were slim.

So I prayed harder and held my breath as the arrow picked up speed on its downward descent.

And it vanished behind the walls of Montségur.

obard threw his arms up in the air and Maryam brought her hands together in a silent clap. I stood awestruck. Robard ducked down and trotted back to us.

"Ha ha!" he said exuberantly when he reached us. "I knew I could make it!"

"Magnificent, Robard, truly a fantastic shot," I said.

We both looked at Maryam, and I expected to see glumness or chagrin on her face, but there was none. In fact she was smiling ear to ear. She made a quick and fluid movement of her arms, and her daggers materialized in her hands.

"Well done, archer. I did not believe you had it in you!" She flipped the daggers in the air, taking each by the blade, and held them out to Robard hilt first. "A wager is a wager. Your choice."

Robard looked at her and smiled. He unstrung his bow, rested the stave on the ground and leaned against it, studying her intently.

"I'm going to need a while to choose. For the time being, you keep them. When I've decided which one I want, I'll let you know. Fair enough?" He looked at her with his head tilted at a jaunty angle.

"As you wish," Maryam said. She spun them in the air again, and they vanished within the folds of her sleeves.

Robard's success gave me a sense of hope. Maybe we could make this work after all.

"What now?" asked Robard.

"I think it's best to wait until dark to attempt the next phase of the plan," I said. "We'll have a better chance of moving about undetected."

Maryam and Robard agreed, and we crept deeper into the woods. We found a dense copse of evergreens where we secreted ourselves. Robard offered to keep the first watch while the rest of us napped. Before we closed our eyes, we shared the remaining bit of food we had left. Ideally we would be inside the castle before it was time for our next meal.

The mountain air was much cooler now. I pulled my tunic tight up around my neck and leaned back against a tree. Before I knew it, Robard was shaking me awake. Darkness had fallen.

I looked up at Robard, confused and still in the twilight of sleep. It had been near dusk when I lay down. He had let me doze much longer than I had intended.

"I thought you needed the rest. Might help you come up with better plans," he said, smiling.

Apparently Robard considered himself a court jester. Still, I was grateful.

"Have you seen anything?" I asked.

"A group of riders came by about two hours ago, but since then, nothing. There is firelight through those trees though. No more than half a league from here, at the base of the trail leading to the southwest wall of the fortress. It's where I'd station my men if I were him."

"We better wake Maryam and get started," I said.

"Are you sure you don't want to reconsider? It's not too late."

"No . . . I made a promise. It wouldn't be right if I didn't try to help. Sir Thomas always taught me that a Templar keeps his word. The order is sworn to protect the weak."

"I wouldn't exactly call Celia weak, and I'm curious as to what you think you can do from inside that the people already there can't. Think this through, squire. If you go any farther, if you get inside, you are committed. If you show yourself to the High Counsel now, your deception is revealed. Just be sure."

Robard was right. I would add to my ever growing list of enemies: Sir Hugh, the King's Guards and King Richard, and, if I helped Celia, the High Counsel. And if he truly was the High Counsel to an archbishop, then he was highly connected to the church and would make a powerful foe. And it also meant he probably knew all the local regimentos of the Templars. He could probably send Sir Hugh straight to me if he so desired.

And there was another thing. Something I hadn't mentioned to either Maryam or Robard. I feared Sir Hugh was closing in on us. There was nothing to base my fear on other than a tickle along the back of my neck. But there were times when I thought that at any moment I would turn my head and he would appear. I was sure of it.

"Let's go," I said.

Robard roused Maryam, and we moved slowly toward the enemy campfire. It was pitch black out with no moon, and the going was slow. The terrain was steep and rough, and more than once we stumbled over the uneven ground and tree roots that fought for purchase in the rocky soil.

It took us the better part of an hour to draw close enough to the fire to get a sense of what we were facing. Their camp was pitched just inside the tree line. The fire was large and sat in a small clearing. We crept closer until we could see the outlines of several men seated and standing about it. I counted twenty, which was about half of the original force. There was no sign of their horses, so they must have had them picketed beyond the fire. We would need to circle around.

We pulled back deeper into the woods and considered our options.

"Where do you suppose the rest of the men are?" Maryam wondered.

"Probably gone with the High Counsel to gather reinforcements," I said. "These few remain here to keep anyone from leaving or entering the castle, until more troops arrive."

We crept back into the trees and circled, always keeping the fire to our left.

"They aren't going to expect anyone, so I'm betting they have a single guard on the horses," Robard whispered.

This turned out to be true. When our eyes readjusted to the darkness, we saw the dim shapes of the horses tethered to a length of rope running between several trees on the far side of their camp. It was a good fifty yards from the fire, so I hoped we could make it away silently.

"How are we going to get rid of the guard?" Robard asked.

"I haven't thought that far ahead yet," I replied. "Give me a minute."

Maryam sighed dramatically, dropping her head, and muttered under her breath, "Only by the grace of Allah have we made it this far." This stung, true as it might be.

"Wait here," she said, and she melted into the night.

"Maryam, hold on!" I whispered. But she was gone.

It was so dark that I could barely see Robard, though he stood only inches away.

"Some girl," he said quietly.

"She is indeed."

We waited in silence, having no idea what to do or if we even had a role in Maryam's plan.

Then very faintly I heard the guard speak.

*"Louis? C'est toi?"* Louis, is that you?

Next came a clunking sound and a groan, followed by the snorts of nervous horses, pawing away. Then in the dim light there was Maryam, frantically untying the animals one by one and turning them loose. I held my breath until she reached the last three in line.

"Come on," I whispered to Robard.

We picked our way through the darkness until we reached the horses.

"Quickly," I said.

We each mounted up. Luckily the High Counsel's knights had not unsaddled.

We guided the horses through the woods and, using the distant fire, tried to steer them through the trees until we could reach the trail. Unfortunately the underbrush grew thickly in this area and in order to reach the castle we would need to pass very near the fire. I found it hard to believe we would escape unseen, and indeed, an instant later, someone saw us trying to quietly pick our way through the darkened forest.

"*Arrêtez! Arrêtez!*" he shouted.

The fire became a clamor of chaos as the soldiers began to shout and jump to their feet, scrambling for their weapons.

"Let's go!" I shouted and kicked at the sides of the horse. The horse bounded forward and Maryam and Robard spurred along right behind. Angel barked, but I concentrated on holding the reins. Bending low in the saddle, I trusted the horse to pick its way through the trees and not run me into a low-hanging branch.

We moved through the very edge of the clearing, and one of the men had wits enough to draw his sword and charge at me. I held tightly to the reins with my left hand and drew the short sword with my right. But, almost comically, Angel charged at the man, barking ferociously, and ran in and around his feet until the man tripped and fell to the ground. A few yards past the clearing, we burst onto the trail and began the steep climb toward the fortress.

I hoped the confusion of the lost horses would give us enough advantage to gain the castle gate before they could catch us.

"Hurry!" I yelled behind me.

We gave free rein to the horses, and once clear of the woods they galloped along the trail. They were used to the rocky terrain and slowed only a little.

We were nearly halfway there when I heard shouts and the approaching hoofbeats of the High Counsel's men. I looked back to find those on foot carrying torches, but it sounded as if a few had managed to find their mounts in the darkness.

Each of us hollered for our horses to go faster, and I grasped the reins as tightly as I could, praying the sprint over the rough ground wouldn't send one of us crashing to our deaths. Ahead I could see a few torches flickering on the battlements of Montségur, as the noise must have attracted the evening guard. I prayed again, hoping Celia had found Robard's arrow and would know what to do.

The wind was stronger out here in the open, and the horse's mane whipped against my face. The gate was only a short distance now. I glanced behind me. It was too dark to see Robard and Maryam, but I heard them shouting encouragement to their steeds. Angel barked as she raced to keep up with us.

With my reins I whipped the horse's flanks, urging him to go faster. More torches lit up the battlements now, and the outline of Montségur was visible in the darkened gloom of the night.

A few seconds later, we were at the castle gate. *"Ouvrez la porte!"* I shouted. Open the door!

"Celia, if you can hear me! It's Tristan! We are here to help, but please open the gate!"

Looking up, I could see torches bobbing to and fro and men shouting, but could not make out what they were saying. We turned our mounts to face the oncoming rush. The men carrying torches were closer now. I was not worried about them because they still had much ground to cover, but the mounted soldiers would arrive at any moment, even though I couldn't yet see them. I strained to hear, but the roar of the wind drowned out their approach.

Robard dismounted, and in the flickering torchlight I could see he had nocked an arrow in his bow. Maryam joined him on the ground, her daggers glinting in the torchlight from the walls.

"Tristan! You had better do something quickly!" Robard shouted as he scanned the trail for targets.

"Celia! Jean-Luc! *Ouvrez la porte!*" I shouted again.

I steered my horse right to the gate and pounded on the thick wooden door with the hilt of my sword.

"Help! We are friends!" I shouted in both English and French.

"Tristan! They're almost here!" Maryam shouted.

Over the noise of the wind and the shouts all around us, I heard the thundering hoofbeats. We were trapped.

Robard loosed an arrow in the darkness and I heard a scream. I dismounted. We would have to make our last stand here at the gates of Montségur.

Robard shot again but missed, and the sound of the horses drew still nearer. I clutched the satchel with my free hand, wishing I had taken Robard's advice and headed home instead of standing where I was now, on a rocky mountaintop about to be run down by my enemies. Then, though it was difficult to hear in all the noise and confusion, the satchel vibrated slightly against my hand, and the musical hum of the Grail reached my ears. I breathed a sigh of relief, but not wishing to tempt fate, hollered again as loudly as I could for someone to please open the door.

Robard, as he was wont, shouted curses at the oncoming soldiers.

"Come and get it, you Frank swine! I'll send you all to the bloody devil!" he shouted over the sound of the approaching riders. I was reasonably sure not one of them understood a word he said.

The wind picked up, but the sound of the breeze couldn't hide the fact that the horsemen were nearly upon us. Robard kept shooting, and even Maryam joined in, shouting out at them in Arabic. How brave they were. Friends I didn't deserve, I thought, chiding myself for bringing them to this place, leading them to their deaths. I hoped the Grail would protect them, save them as it had saved Maryam on the ship. Please, God, I prayed. Don't let my friends die.

And my prayer was answered by the groaning sound of the castle door as it swung slowly open.

# 16

obard, Maryam! The door!"

With a shuddering creak the wooden door pushed open just wide enough for a person to slip inside. Inside, Jean-Luc held a torch in one hand and shouted, *"Pressez!"* Hurry! Robard didn't hear him, as he was lustily shouting and shooting at the oncoming men. I grabbed Maryam by the arm and shoved her through the door.

"Robard! It's open!" I shouted.

"Want another, you fleas on a Frank dog's arse? Show this one to your pompous cow of a High Counsel!" he shouted as he loosed yet another arrow.

Jean-Luc stepped through the door, and in the light of his torch I could see Robard reaching for his wallet, but I leapt forward and grabbed his arm.

"Robard! We have to go now!" Something whizzed by my head, and a crossbow bolt thunked into the wood of the door behind me. I pulled at Robard, and Angel barked at him furiously, either because he was unnecessarily risking his life or because she was angry at his mention of fleas. Robard released one final shot, and then we all darted through the gate to safety. The door moaned shut and I could hear the horses and the men outside shouting. The sounds of bolts and battle-axes thumped against the gate.

Robard, Maryam and I slumped, bent over with our hands on our knees, trying to catch our breath. The sounds of the High Counsel's men eventually retreated.

The interior of Montségur was lit by torches. A few yards away, a large bonfire cast a glimmering light off the rocks and bricks of the walls. I heard a voice I recognized in an instant.

"Hello, Templar," she said.

When I first looked at her, something happened to my heart. I'm not sure what, for nothing like it had ever happened to me. It seemed to stop beating momentarily, then started again as if in a rush to catch up. My breath wouldn't come, and I told myself it was because I was winded from the ride and all the excitement outside the gate. But I knew it wasn't true.

She was dressed simply, in a cream-colored tunic falling well below her knees. My eyes were drawn to hers. I remembered their icy blueness. If anything, the intervening days had drawn them an even deeper shade. Her auburn hair fell loose about her shoulders and framed a heart-shaped face. Her skin glowed in the firelight, and looking at her made me feel like I had taken a long drink of cool spring water.

"I . . . We . . . Hello, Celia," I stammered. Time had slowed. I couldn't move, and could barely speak.

"I knew it," Maryam whispered to Robard, who nodded emphatically. Angel was overjoyed to find Celia there. She ran to her, and Celia knelt to scratch her behind the ears, smiling. "Hello, little Angel," she said.

"So I take it you got our message? I hope no one was hurt," I finally said.

She reached out her hand, and the light reflected off Sir Thomas' Templar ring. I took it from her and she smiled.

"Message received, and no harm done," she said. She greeted Robard and Maryam.

"Welcome to Montségur," she said. "Please allow me to extend all hospitality. Jean-Luc, I'm sure they must be hungry and tired. Can you see they are fed and have a place to sleep?" She spoke these words in French, but slowly, so I could follow along. My face fell, though, for after everything we had gone through to get here, I had no wish to leave Celia's company so soon.

"I am not . . . Robard and Maryam may be . . . I'm not hungry, thank you," I finally spat out. Celia's presence severely limited my ability to speak. In fact, I was starving, but I decided on the spot to give up food forever if it meant remaining in Celia's presence.

"Come along, Robard. I'm sure Tristan has much to discuss with Celia. Let us find a place to rest. We could both use it." Maryam took Robard gently by the arm and followed Jean-Luc into a darkened corner of the courtyard. We were finally alone.

"Why did you come here, Templar?" she asked.

She got right to the point.

"It wasn't our original plan. We left our camp and headed south to the beach, intending to head to Perpignan and find a ship. But we encountered your friend the High Counsel . . ."

"He is no friend of mine!" she interrupted.

"Yes, so I gathered. He's a rather unpleasant fellow. At any rate, we convinced him that you had headed to Perpignan, to throw him off your trail. And according to Robard, he did go there, but quickly learned you and your party had not been seen there and returned to track you here."

"How did Robard know all of this?"

"It's a long story and not terribly exciting, I'm afraid."

"As you can see," she said, sweeping her arms in a wide circle, "I have nothing but time."

"Let's just say we split up for a while, but we all reconnected and now we're here."

"I see."

"I just felt I should try to help, if I could," I said. The details were unimportant. She undoubtedly had more important matters on her mind.

"It was good of you to come, Templar, and we can certainly use your help, but I fear you are now trapped here with us for a while."

We didn't say anything else for a few moments, which I spent trying not to stare at Celia. But she had her hair pushed up off her face with a headband, and the way the firelight reflected off her held me transfixed.

"Celia, there is more, something else I must tell you."

"Yes?" She looked at me expectantly.

"We met up with Philippe. He . . . When we found him . . ." I couldn't tell her.

"Out with it, Templar."

"He didn't make it. Philippe is dead. He single-handedly fought six of the High Counsel's men and managed to kill four of them before he died. We . . . Robard, Maryam and I, we encountered . . . and took care of the other two." One of them, at least, permanently.

Grief washed over Celia's face in a wave. Her eyes moistened instantly.

"I'm so sorry for your loss," I said.

She nodded in thanks, but said nothing. A single tear left her eye and rolled gently down her cheek. My brain told my arm to reach out then. To embrace her and wipe the tear away. But I did not. My arm felt frozen in place.

"I wish I could . . ." I stopped, for my words sounded empty even to me. I felt useless, standing there like a statue, unable to comfort her.

"Poor Philippe," she finally said.

"Had he served your father long?" I asked, desperate for her to talk or do anything but cry.

"Since I was a child. My father wished for Philippe and I to marry."

Her words hit me like a hammer to the stomach. She was to marry Philippe? I had thought, by the way they acted together, with her clearly in charge, that their relationship was adversarial if nothing else.

"Really? Then I am doubly sorry," I said, not meaning a word of it. I was instantly aware that I was guilty of the sin of jealousy, but I would ask forgiveness later.

"Yes. It was my father's wish, not mine. I am . . . was . . . fond of Philippe, but I had no desire to marry him."

"I see," I said, trying to keep the joy out of my voice. But my happiness was immediately replaced by guilt, when I remembered that the poor man had bravely given his life for her. What had become of me? What were these feelings that consumed me? Right then I was further crushed by the loss of Sir Thomas. I wished he were there. Or Sir Basil, or Quincy. I wished I could talk to them about this woman who made me feel so strange.

Celia was quiet, to gather herself.

"Celia, would you like me to go with you to tell your father about Philippe?" I offered.

She shook her head. "No, thank you, but my father is not here. When I went to conference with the archbishop, my father left for Paris to petition the King for help. He won't return for some time."

This was not good news. I had assumed Celia's father would be in command of his men-at-arms. Jean-Luc acted capable, but Philippe had said he had very little experience, and he was not much older than me. I silently cursed my luck. My talent for placing myself in dangerous and nearly hopeless situations apparently knew no bounds.

"Thank you for coming back, Templar, and for being there with Philippe at the end. I know he loved me, and though I could not return those feelings, he was a good man, a loyal servant to my father and a fierce protector of our people. When this is over, we shall celebrate his life as is our way, but if Philippe were here now, he would say, 'First things first.' Come. Let me find you a hot meal and a bed. You must be exhausted."

"Celia, about Philippe. When I found him, he was very near death. I promised him a Christian burial, but he insisted I not waste the time. He demanded I come to you immediately. I hope it was the right thing."

She smiled and closed her eyes, lost in some pleasant memory. "It was, Tristan. You did exactly the right thing. Do not worry. I know our beliefs may sound strange to you. But we are a simple people, devout in our own way. You did exactly as Philippe would have wished. Come let me show you our fortress."

She held out her hand for me to take. I stood there, unable to move any part of my body. She looked down at her hand, then up at my face and quietly laughed. She finally took my hand in hers, and I couldn't be certain, but a bolt of lightning may have traveled directly from my hand to my brain. She took a torch from a sconce on the wall nearest us and led me across the courtyard to an area beneath the battlements where several cook fires still blazed. A few men and women busied about, cooking and talking cheerfully to one another. At a command from Celia, a plate of simmering meat and vegetables was placed in my hand.

The aroma was so enticing that it took every ounce of my self-control not to devour the entire portion in one gulp. However, I would need to let go of her hand to eat, and I had no wish to do so. Standing there, feeling temporarily safe and happy, I voted for starvation over severing our physical connection. But she released my hand and sat on a nearby barrel so I could eat.

When I had finished the meal, Celia led me up a set of stairs to a second level of the castle keep, then down a corridor to a small room with no door.

"Our accommodations are not elegant, but they will have to do." She placed the torch in a holder on the wall. The room was indeed small and windowless, with only a straw mattress on the floor, but it was much better than sleeping directly on the cold stone.

"This will do me fine," I said. "Where are Maryam and Robard?"

"They are down the hall, in their own rooms. I'm sure they're fast asleep by now. All of you must be exhausted. We'll talk more in the morning," she said as she moved to leave.

"Celia, wait, I have many questions," I said. Actually I had very few, but I did not wish her to leave. She smiled at me.

"Tomorrow," she said softly, and drifted away down the hall.

So I slept, collapsing to the mattress and not even moving until Robard nudged me awake with his boot.

"Rise, squire. The High Counsel has returned and there's something else you need to see," he said, anticipation tinged with apprehension in his voice.

"What is it?" I groused, for I had not rested well. Dreams of Celia, pleasant though they were, had intruded on my sleep and woken me several times during the night. Now fully awake, I felt tired and out of sorts.

"You'll see," he said, turning toward the door. "Hurry."

Robard led me back to the bailey, and I squinted in the bright sun as we left the dimness of the keep. He bounded farther up the stairs to the battlements atop Montségur's walls, and shortly we stood above the southwest gate.

"What is it?" I asked again.

"Look for yourself." He pointed to the field below us, rocky and steep. I peered out, shocked at how many more of the High Counsel's men had joined his original force. There were at least several hundred men mounted near the tree line. I located him at the head of the column, moving onto the field below the castle, his horse prancing along and his cape flowing behind him. To his immediate rear rode the color bearer carrying a large green-and-white flag, and next to him, a rider carried another banner: the familiar brown-and-white Templar flag.

Suddenly, nothing made sense. Why would the High Counsel

have a Templar regimento with him? My eyes traveled back to where he sat upon his stallion, and I recognized the rider next to him instantly. The meal I'd eaten the night before roiled in my stomach, and I thought for a moment I might be sick on the spot.

Sir Hugh.

## 17

E ven though I knew he would never stop trying to find me, a small part of me had prayed that something would delay Sir Hugh. Bad weather, a wayward arrow, poison, anything. But he had managed to crush even that small hope.

"How? How does he do it? He escapes from Acre, a city overrun by Saracens, he follows us across an ocean and survives a storm that sinks our ship, and now he finds us here in the middle of nowhere, stuck in a tiny castle! Has he given his soul to Satan, just for the privilege of thwarting me at every turn?" I muttered on longer until I had nothing left to say. Though I was not as experienced at cursing as Robard, I ran through every one I knew. Sir Hugh. A snake, a weasel and a polecat all rolled into one.

If I hadn't known better, I would've said Robard was amused by my futile rant. "What now?" he asked. The steel in his voice brought me back into focus. Robard had a look in his eyes I had noticed before in our time together. Despite his frequent protests, and his genuine desire to return home, he loved a fight. Especially if it involved teaching a harsh lesson to a couple of pompous jackasses like Sir Hugh and the High Counsel. Yet he was also a realist.

"This changes things. Your friend the High Counsel might have eventually given up the siege. I doubt we can say the same about your friend Sir Hugh," he said.

He was right, of course. We were locked in, and I knew Sir Hugh would kill every last man, woman and child here in order to get the Grail. I had foolishly trapped us in this fortress, and now we would pay a heavy price trying to get out of it. To Robard's credit he did not remind me that he had counseled against such a move in the first place.

"Do you think he can be bought off?" Robard asked.

"How?"

"With whatever it is you're carrying. Think about it. Give him what he wants and it's over."

Robard did not understand. Giving Sir Hugh the Grail would not save our lives. He'd kill us all anyway so no one else would know he had it. It wouldn't be over until I had delivered the Grail safely to Father William at Rosslyn or until Sir Hugh or I were dead.

"Robard . . . I can't. I swore an oath to Sir Thomas. If you had given a vow to your father, would you break it?"

Robard said nothing for a while, looking out at the ground below the fortress.

"Oaths are funny things, Tristan. Some are worth dying for, I'll grant you. Your people, your family, even your country sometimes. Some, though, become more than the giver can bear. My father swore his fealty to King Henry, and what did it get him? When Henry died, his sniveling son took over"—Robard paused to spit at the mention of King Richard—"and everything my father fought and bled for was suddenly meaningless. You are my friend. I've come to trust you, like I've trusted few before. So I ask you, is what you carry worth dying for?"

"Sir Thomas thought so," I said.

"I never met Sir Thomas, so I don't know what kind of man he was. You swear by his memory, so I'll take you at your word. But even if he were alive and standing here before me, I'm not asking him. I'm asking you. Is what you carry worth dying for?"

Robard's question made me think long and hard before I answered. Sir Thomas believed it with all his heart. He entrusted it to me, and from what I had witnessed of the Grail so far, I knew I would die before I let Sir Hugh possess it.

"Yes, Robard, it is."

"Then that is enough for me. I'll see you through this, Tristan. Until you tell me it's done."

I was so moved by Robard's words that I couldn't speak. Something about him had changed since he'd returned to us in the village below. He was still headstrong and temperamental, of course, but calmer. He had committed to something he didn't fully understand, but maybe here among his new friends he had found a struggle worthy of his gifts—unlike his experience in Outremer, which had only left him bitter and angry.

"Why the sudden change of heart? Before this you wanted only to get to England. Now it's quite possible we won't get out of here alive. Why?"

"Because you are my friend," he said. He left me then. This was his final word on the matter. In his own way, Robard had sworn an oath, and I felt better than I had in days.

I stood there alone, the wind hitting my face. It was a cool morning and the breeze had picked up. I heard movement behind me but didn't turn.

"Tell me what you see," Celia said to me.

"Trouble," I replied.

To my surprise, she laughed.

"We certainly have no shortage of that here," she said.

"So it would seem."

She stood beside me and closed her eyes.

"I love the feel of wind in my hair, don't you?" she asked me.

"I don't know. I've never really thought about it before." And I wasn't thinking about it now. I stared at her, and despite our circumstances, she looked peaceful, almost serene.

"Really?" she answered. "All the time you grew up in a monastery, contemplating God and his miracles, and you never once stopped to feel a breeze on your face? What did you do all day?"

"Mostly worked," I replied. "There were always chores. I'm not sure the abbot would have found 'contemplating the feel of the wind' a worthwhile use of time."

"Hmph. Sounds like a very ill-mannered man."

"Not really. Stern. But fair. Brilliant even, in many ways."

"I've yet to meet any cleric whom I would consider brilliant. Bigoted. Prejudiced. Judgmental. I've met many of those."

"I can't argue. I can only say that the monks who raised me were kind. Industrious to be sure, but I never wanted for anything."

"What about your parents? Didn't you wish to know who they were?"

"Of course. But the monks had no control over that. They simply took me in."

"I'm sorry. It was rude of me to question the motives of men

I've never met. I just . . . We've been so unfairly persecuted by the church. It's hard to remember my manners sometimes."

I let it pass without comment. Truthfully, I was more concerned about the troops lining up below us than I was about Celia's feelings about the church or the brothers.

"Celia, there is something I must tell you. There are Templars on the field below. The High Counsel has enlisted their aid. Their Marshal is known to me. His name is Sir Hugh Monfort. In truth, he is here for me."

"After you? Why? Are you not allies?"

"No. Sir Hugh was . . . is a dreadful man. He has committed many violations of our laws. My liege Sir Thomas wrote testimony against him, including sworn statements by many brother knights of our regimento. He entrusted me to deliver them to the Master of the Order in England. I barely made it out of Acre, but Sir Hugh followed me. He's been chasing me ever since."

I then told her the rest of my story, leaving out only Sir Thomas giving me the Grail. She listened intently while I told her about meeting King Richard in Dover, and how I had seen Sir Hugh outside the Commandery meeting with the King's Guards. And how the King's Guards had followed me the next day through the marketplace in Dover.

"In Acre, before I left, I had an encounter with one of the King's Guards in the stables. He was one of those who had followed me in Dover, and I questioned him about it. He lied and said he didn't know me, but I pressed him further and he drew his sword. Only the timely arrival of the King stopped us from injuring each other."

"The King intervened?" she asked.

"Yes. Yet, when I think about it now, he had a strange look

on his face. As if he were reluctant to stop it. He had to have ordered his guards to follow me in Dover. They answer to no one else but him. But why? And then in Acre, if I hadn't saved his life on the battlefield, I'm certain . . ."

"Wait," she interrupted, reaching out and resting her hand on my forearm. "You rescued Richard the Lionheart?" Her touch made me feel dizzy, and I took hold of the stone parapet with my free hand, afraid I might pitch over the side if I didn't anchor myself.

"Yes. It was nothing, really. I just gave him my horse and he returned to the rear. He is reckless in battle. For a king. Anyway, finding me there in the stable, he looked torn. Almost as if he would be relieved to have his guard strike me down."

Celia's mouth formed a straight line as she concentrated on the details of my story. "I wonder what Richard finds so fascinating about you."

"I don't know. It's all very strange." Trumpets sounded, and the shouts of orders to the men-at-arms and knights traveled over the ground below us, drawing my attention to the field.

"Which one is this Sir Hugh?" she asked. I pointed him out.

"How could he have known you survived the storm and were shipwrecked?" she asked.

"He couldn't. But he wouldn't have taken any chances. I'm sure he pursued our ship and tracked behind the storm. When the storm hit land, he simply followed and is being thorough. He's no doubt had knights and sergeantos scouring the countryside asking everyone if travelers fitting our descriptions have been in the area. He must have learned we'd crossed paths with the High Counsel and is here to help him. I'm sure by now he's convinced the High Counsel we are also heretics. Evil as he is, he has the most alarming good fortune. It's almost as if we've been delivered to him on a platter."

"Whoever he is, he'll find it hard to get in here. We have plenty of food and water to survive a long siege," she said confidently.

"I do not wish for my troubles to confound your problems, Celia. The first chance I get, I'll try to sneak away and . . ."

Celia held up her hand. "Nonsense. I won't hear of it. You and your friends may stay here as long as you need to."

"But I'm afraid, Celia. Afraid for all of you. With Sir Hugh here now . . ." I stopped and looked out at the still assembling troops. By counting the battle flags, I estimated there were close to five hundred men.

"Celia, how many are sheltered here behind the walls?"

"There are nearly three hundred. Mostly women and children."

I winced. "How many fighting men?"

"Jean-Luc leads my father's fyrd now with Philippe gone. He has fifteen well-trained and well-armed men. The rest are farmers or merchants, I would guess seventy in all."

I tried to hide my dismay but I couldn't blame Celia. Most every fyrd is just a band of volunteers, loyal to their lord. They train a few times a year and fight if need be, but they are not professional soldiers. This was bad; fewer than one hundred men, most of them not even soldiers, against an army of five hundred. Those were truly awful odds, even with the high ground and the fortress on our side. If Sir Hugh were determined enough, he would throw his men at the walls until we were overrun.

"Do you have weapons?" I asked.

"Yes. Come, I will show you to our armory," she said.

We were about to leave but were distracted by shouts from the field below. Looking down, we saw Sir Hugh and the High Counsel riding up toward the castle gate almost below where we stood.

In the High Counsel's left hand he held aloft a white flag, and he waved it back and forth.

They wished to talk.

# 18

ow what do we do?" she asked.

I needed a minute to think. Talking to Sir Hugh and the High Counsel might actually be a good idea. After all, they each had a different agenda. I wondered if I could play them against each other.

"Celia, do Jean-Luc and his men have crossbows?"

"Yes, of course," she said.

I would have preferred longbows, but I knew the French generally did not use them in battle. A pity. I could station Robard on the wall, but I wanted him to come with me to the parley.

"Please find Jean-Luc and have his men span their crossbows and stand ready on the battlement here above the gate. I'll summon Robard and Maryam, and we will see what they have to say. Agreed?"

Celia nodded and left while I scanned the courtyard below for Robard. He and Maryam were seated near the cooking fire, deep in conversation. Angel lay curled at Maryam's feet, working feverishly on a bone. I scampered down a ladder and ran across the courtyard to them.

"Sir Hugh and the High Counsel are outside under a flag of truce. I'd like you and Maryam to come with me and Celia to find out what they want," I said.

"Will I get to shoot someone?" Robard asked hopefully.

"Maybe later," I said. "We'll talk first."

"How can we trust him?" Maryam asked.

"Celia is having Jean-Luc assemble men with crossbows on the wall. We'll be well within range."

"Hmph. Crossbows. Tell those Franks when the shooting starts not to hit us!" Robard exclaimed.

"I'm sure it will be fine, Robard. Let's go," I said. Angel jumped up to join us, but I bade her stay, and she returned to her bone.

We waited at the gate until Celia returned with Jean-Luc and his men. He ordered them to the battlement above us and gave me a small salute when they were ready.

Before we left, I felt the need to say something. "Celia, I don't feel right making all of these decisions, but we should come to some agreement about who will direct our defense and speak to Sir Hugh and the High Counsel."

"I think it falls to you, Templar," she said.

"What? Why? I'm just a squire, I have no . . ."

She interrupted me. "Jean-Luc is barely older than you. He is a good man, but inexperienced. The rest of the men-at-arms serve only because my father pays them well. They will do what he says, and he will follow my orders. When I tell him you are in charge, you will have no trouble with Jean-Luc," she said plainly.

"This is not a good idea," I said. Maryam and Robard watched our exchange with bemused expressions on their faces.

"Why not? You have been to war. You just told me how you rescued a king on the battlefield. You were obviously clever enough to devise a way into our fortress. I would say that makes you more than qualified. Remember, these are farmers. My father has them train for battle once or twice a year. You're the logical choice."

I couldn't agree. "Robard, you are a King's Archer. You have a great deal more experience than me. You should be the one . . ."

Robard shook his head. "Not really, squire. I'm an archer. Mostly I stood behind every skirmish and launched arrows into the air. I'm *willing* to fight these bas— uh, anyone, but I don't know anything about commanding troops." He smiled. Drat.

"But I—" I started to say.

"Tristan, didn't you tell us about your knight Sir Thomas and how he feverishly directed the defense of Acre?" Robard asked.

"Yes?"

"And you watched and learned and trained with him every day for more than a year, true?" he went on.

"Yes."

"We are in a similar situation. Think of what he did and try to apply the same tactics here," Robard offered, as if it were easy. And I decided to ignore the fact that despite Sir Thomas' best efforts, Acre had been lost. I would not give in so easily to their demands.

"Maryam, you are a member of Al Hashshashin, and you . . ." She never let me finish.

"Oh no, not me, Templar. We fight in small groups, attacking quickly and then withdrawing. I've never even been in a castle before now," she said. If I hadn't known better, despite the danger we were in, I could have sworn she and Robard were enjoying themselves. They glanced back and forth at each other with smiling eyes and looked as if they might burst out laughing at any moment. Or maybe something else was going on between them. For the past few days I had caught them staring at each other when each thought the other wasn't looking.

"There you have it," Celia said. "Glad it's all settled now. You shall command our defenses. It's decided." She started toward the gate.

"Hold it!" I said. "This is folly. I'm no . . . I can't . . . If you put me in charge, we're doomed!"

Robard shrugged. "We're doomed anyway," he said. He brushed past me toward the gate. "Let's go see what they have to say."

I followed meekly along, wondering how this had happened and convinced this was not a good idea. Then I asked God to please send Celia's father home quickly.

Two men guarded the gate, and together they lifted the heavy timber crossbeam that held the door locked in place. It slowly swung open and the four of us stepped through it, my stomach lurching when I heard it slam shut. I didn't like feeling so exposed.

The High Counsel and Sir Hugh sat astride their mounts about thirty yards from the gate. The four of us fanned out, with Celia and Maryam in the middle and Robard and I on the ends. Robard held his bow, already strung in his left hand, and Maryam had her hands up inside her sleeves, pretending to be warming her hands against the cool air, but no doubt gripping her daggers. And while I nervously fingered my short sword, Celia wore no weapon I could see. We marched forward in silence, stopping about ten yards shy of the two men.

The High Counsel's mount was a solid-black stallion, which pranced nervously and threw its head about in the stiffening wind.

He had to work the reins to keep it still, but this did not stop him from sending a dark look toward Celia.

"Hello, Princess," he said.

Princess?

"Father Renard," she replied coldly. "I see you have made a new friend," she said, turning to stare at Sir Hugh. But Sir Hugh ignored her as his eyes bore into me.

"As have you," the High Counsel replied, looking at me. "I thought I warned you about what would happen if you sought to aid these heretics."

"You did. But you also lied. You called them bandits first, then heretics, remember?" Robard interrupted. The High Counsel gave him a long silent stare before he spoke.

"What I called them matters little. They *are* heretics and enemies of the church!" he said.

"One man's heresy is another man's faith, wouldn't you say?" Robard shot back.

"Silence! I do not debate theology with heretics!" Father Renard shouted.

"Now *I'm* a heretic?" Robard goaded, arching an eyebrow at the priest. "You only just met me!"

Father Renard ignored him and spoke again to Celia. "You can end this now, girl. Surrender yourself to me and I will withdraw my men. We will return to Languedoc for your trial." Sir Hugh shot a sideways glance at the High Counsel that told me this was not what they had agreed to.

"Leave with me now, or face the consequences," Father Renard continued.

"No," I said.

Sir Hugh hissed something at Father Renard and they backed their horses up a few yards. They argued with each other, but we could not hear what was said.

"Something wrong, Sir Hugh?" I asked. He swung his horse around with a flourish and cantered back to his earlier spot.

"If it isn't the world's luckiest squire," he hissed.

"Nice of you to come," I said, bowing slightly.

"It must be a *miracle* you survived the storm," he said. "Yes. You're very lucky. In fact, I was on my way out of this valley when I encountered one of the High Counsel's men. He described a fight he had with three travelers. Even claimed an archer murdered his companion! So perhaps your luck has taken a turn for the worse," he sneered, and shot Robard a very dark look.

"A heretic and a murderer? This is quite a day I'm having," Robard exclaimed. "Are there any sins left for me to commit? Treason, perhaps?"

Sir Hugh ignored Robard and returned his eyes to me. "I have made an agreement with the good Father," he went on. "I will align my forces with his temporarily, and together we will destroy this fortress and your little band of farmers and rabble. When we are done, Father Renard can do whatever he wishes with the girl and your two *friends*," he spat, pointing toward Maryam and Robard, "but you're mine, squire. All mine." Sir Hugh's eyes took on a peculiar glaze, almost as if he was dreaming of the joy my demise would bring him.

"We're not afraid of you, Sir Hugh. If you think so, come ahead." This time it was my turn to look at the High Counsel. "Ask Sir Hugh, Father. He will tell you God is most definitely on *our* side."

Sir Hugh started to reply, but the High Counsel held up his hand.

"Enough of this. Princess, I give you one hour . . ."

"You give them *nothing!*" Sir Hugh yelled at Father Renard, who was so startled he nearly tumbled from his saddle. "I am Marshal of the Knights Templar. Who do you answer to?"

"What? I . . . Why . . . I answer to the Archbishop of Languedoc . . . ," Father Renard stammered.

"And who does he answer to?" Sir Hugh yelled back, pulling his mount closer and closer to the High Counsel.

"He answers to His Holiness Celestine III, of course," he said, trying not to show fear.

"Excellent! Then you should know, Father Renard, as a Templar Knight my order answers *directly* to His Holiness. Do you understand me? You and your men are here at my command! And you will not negotiate with these . . . peasants . . . unless I give you permission! Is that understood!"

"No, it is most definitely not understood!" the High Counsel shouted. "This was not our agreement . . . You promised . . . ," but before he could finish, Sir Hugh drew his sword. His blade glinted in the sunlight as he swung it around, stopping it just inches short of the High Counsel's neck.

Shock registered in Father Renard's eyes and he reared back in his saddle, struggling to maintain his balance. He finally regained his seat, staring at Sir Hugh, his eyes wide. Then he glanced down at the gleaming blade and the color drained from his face.

"What are you doing?" he sputtered. "This was not our agreement!"

Sir Hugh flicked his wrist and his sword nicked the flesh on the Father's neck. A small rivulet of blood trickled down, running beneath the collar of his tunic.

"I'm altering the terms! I care not what you want or who you think you are," Sir Hugh snarled. "Do you understand me? Swear fealty to me *now* or I will strike you down this instant!"

The High Counsel's eyes rolled and darted. He looked at Celia, then me, but he had nowhere to go. The confident, even arrogant man who had confronted us on the beach was gone. The mad knight who held the sword to his neck was more than his match. He had made a terrible miscalculation and now had no way out.

"Sir Hugh! Please, there is no need for violence . . . I was only . . . ," the High Counsel sputtered.

"I disagree!" Sir Hugh shouted. "I feel a very great need for violence! So, priest, what will it be? Swear to me!" He moved his sword again, and the High Counsel squeaked as the point cut deeper into his flesh.

Father Renard waved his arms, and behind him a group of his men broke ranks and started toward the parley. One of the High Counsel's men spurred his horse and lowered his lance as if to charge. "Brothers!" Sir Hugh shouted, and as he did, three Templars mounted several yards behind him spun their steeds and rode to intercept the charging knight.

"What is going on?" Robard whispered. His right hand held an arrow loosely nocked in the string of his bow, and made to raise it and take aim.

"Hold, Robard," I said quietly. "We may need to run for the gate. We'll need those arrows then."

The High Counsel's knight was no match for the superior horsemanship of the Templars. Without even lowering lances, they steered the High Counsel's man away and drove him back toward the lines. No help was coming for Father Renard.

Sir Hugh sat up in his saddle and pushed his sword deeper into Father Renard's neck. If he moved or his horse spooked, the High Counsel would likely die. He breathed heavily, and despite the cold air and wind, sweat rolled from his forehead and down his neck, where it mixed with the blood that now flowed steadily from his wound. Sir Hugh was not wearing his helmet, and his long hair and scraggly beard flew about in the breeze. The effect made him look completely insane. He was a lost soul. Completely mad.

"Now. *Father* Renard." He spat out the words. "Do you swear to follow my orders? To live and die at my command? In the name of His Holiness?"

Celia and Maryam had spent the last few seconds backing cautiously toward the gate. They were both poised and ready to run at the slightest provocation. I slowly moved my hand to my sword, taking firm hold of the hilt. "Steady now," I whispered. I feared if we broke and ran, Sir Hugh and his men might ride us down. He was just crazy enough to take on a battlement full of crossbowmen.

Something had changed in him since Tyre. When pressed in battle or confronted by an enemy who was his equal, he was an unrepentant coward. As a bully he knew no peer. But here he had taken on someone who could decide to fight back. He had the advantage in numbers certainly. But he was desperate now. If the High Counsel did not yield, Sir Hugh may attempt to strike us all down, and I realized what a mistake I had made in agreeing to meet outside the walls of Montségur. The next move belonged to Father Renard.

"Yes. Of course. Forgive me." The High Counsel stumbled over his words.

"What was that?" Sir Hugh said. "I'm afraid I didn't hear you!"

"I said I was mistaken. You are clearly in charge. What is it you wish to do, sire?"

The sword went in again, and the High Counsel winced. His head leaned toward his shoulder as if he could squeeze the sword away. Sir Hugh moved and twisted the point to further torment the man.

"Did I not ask you to *swear!*" he hissed at Father Renard.

"I swear! I swear all my men and loyalty to you, Sir Hugh! In the name of God, without question!" For good measure he made the sign of the cross. I didn't realize I'd been holding my breath, but it came out of my lungs in a rush. I gave a prayer of thanks to God for making Father Renard a coward also.

With blinding speed, Sir Hugh withdrew his sword and smiled his serpent's smile. "Excellent!" he said, returning the sword to its sheath.

"Are you mad, Sir Hugh?" I asked. He had just displayed his insanity quite clearly for everyone to see, but I could think of nothing else to say.

"Let me shoot him!" Robard pleaded under his breath.

"You'd better not miss, archer!" Sir Hugh sneered. Apparently he had ears like a hare. He gave rein to his stallion and it pranced back and forth. "I'll ride you down and kill you before you pull another arrow."

"Get out of here, Sir Hugh," I sneered. "Leave now."

Father Renard sat despondently on his horse, hand clutched at his bleeding neck. When he wiped away the blood, the cut showed, and it crudely resembled a Templar cross. He would wear a scar there for the rest of his days. His face was crestfallen. Beaten and humili-ated by Sir Hugh, he finally stared at me. And for yet one more time, I saw myself looking into the eyes of an enemy. A gaze filled with the purest form of hatred. I was to blame for his misfortune.

"Hear this, Templar! Leave no doubt in your tiny little brain," Sir Hugh shouted. "You have one hour. Then you surrender your-self at this very spot. If you do not yield, you will be overrun and I will give no quarter." He didn't wait for us to answer but galloped back toward his men.

The Father remained behind. He tried to stare me down, but I did not waver.

"I warned you," he rasped. "I explained to you what would happen if you deceived me! Make ready, Princess. Pray you die in battle, Templar, for if I meet you on the field, you will know no mercy!"

"I think you'll have to ask Sir Hugh's permission first," I said. "He seems to think my death belongs to him alone."

"Make light all you wish, heretic! You will not live past this day! I *swear* it."

He turned then, but Robard called to him. "Father!" He stopped and turned his horse to face us again.

"Your neck is bleeding," Robard said.

Robard gave him a jaunty little salute and Father Renard whipped his horse and rode back to his lines. He made a point of steering his stallion away from Sir Hugh, who stood conferring with some of the Templar Knights.

Beads of sweat rolled down my brow as I realized we had only an hour to ready ourselves for an assault by several hundred experienced fighters. Already in the tree line below the open plain, I could hear the sound of axes. I was sure trees were being cut and scaling ladders were under construction, possibly for a catapult or some other type of siege engine.

"Come on. Let's go," I said.

We returned to the fortress and discussed our options.

"What do we do now?" Maryam asked. "We're severely outnumbered."

"We've been besieged before. Montségur has never fallen," Celia replied confidently.

"Celia, with all due respect, I do not think this will be like other sieges," I said. She shrugged in reply.

"Agreed," Robard cut in. "Can Jean-Luc show me to the armory?"

"Yes, of course." She motioned to Jean-Luc, who led Robard away.

"I would suggest you tell your subjects to make ready," I told her.

Celia's eyes sparked in anger. "They are not my subjects!" Her quick turn of mood gave Maryam leave to trail after Robard and Jean-Luc, and we were left alone.

"I did not mean to make you angry. But the High Counsel did call you Princess."

"As you once said, Templar, it is a long and not very exciting story."

"I have time," I retorted, though I most certainly did not.

She let out a heavy sigh. "My father was once a duke. Loyal to King Philip. He was one of the nobles who fought with Philip to unite the kingdom. But when he embraced Catharism, his titles and most of his lands were stripped from him by the church, with Philip's tacit approval. Technically, I am . . . or was . . . nobly born. Not anymore. Although if the High Counsel had had his way . . ." She let the words trail off.

"Way with what? Had his way with what?" Impatience clouded my words.

Celia fidgeted. "I suppose you might as well know. When we went to the council with the archbishop, he offered a solution. If I would marry Father Renard and renounce Catharism, thereby solidifying the archbishop's grip on my father and his lands, he would intercede with the King to restore our lands and title. When I refused, he declared us heretics, and ordered us to stand trial. Philippe arranged our escape. It is why Father Renard came after me." She paused a moment, for the memory of Philippe brought her sadness.

"Marry a priest?" I asked. I had lived with monks all my life. Such a thought had never occurred to me.

Celia smiled and nodded. "Yes, he would leave the church and become a duke, of course remaining loyal to the archbishop." I shrugged. This was all to complicated for me to think about. There were other much more important matters to attend to.

"Celia, what happened at the council, this siege, you are blameless. Philippe's death is not your fault. He was a soldier who died doing his duty. But I am sorry for bringing Father Renard and Sir Hugh together, for I feel I've only made it worse."

Celia seemed possessed of an unbreakable spirit. She considered my words a moment, then nodded. "So, Templar, what do you suggest we do now?"

"Is there any chance your father might return here soon?"

"There is no way to know. He is certainly in Paris by now, but it all depends on whether or even if Philip will give him an audience. He needed to pay a sizable sum of money for a 'trial,' and if Philip rules against him . . ." Her words trailed off, and I could sense the worry she had for her father. I had heard the monks speak of this practice before. A noble could petition the King for a ruling on some matter, usually involving lands or titles, but was required to pay a hefty amount of money for the King's or lord's time. It was an easy way for monarchs to collect vast sums of wealth and pay for their armies.

It didn't matter now, but I had hoped her father was somewhere nearby and could send aid. Something along the lines of a thousand mounted knights would certainly be welcome. My friends had chosen me to lead them. Foolish though they may have been, it was past time for me to act.

"There are more than five hundred men out there determined to have this fortress for a trophy. Gather your folk and tell them what is coming. Get every able-bodied man and adult woman on the battlements, even the young boys. If they are old enough to carry water or lift a pitchfork, we need them. Move the younger children inside the keep and have a few of the elders watch over them. Take Angel with you. She will help keep the children occupied. But do it quickly. And have everyone clear the bailey. We have no idea what they may throw at us."

Celia hurried toward the keep while I climbed to the parapet again. As I feared, several long, straight logs were being pulled into sight. Crossbeams would be lashed to them, making them into scaling ladders. I tried to think like Sir Thomas would and considered our advantages. We held the high ground behind thick stone walls.

The trail up to the castle from the tree line was steep, rocky and narrow. It would not be easy to mount a charge, and any assault could come from only one direction, as the fortress backed up to sheer rock walls. We were outnumbered and, more than likely, at a disadvantage with weapons. Sir Hugh would certainly construct a siege engine or two. It was unlikely they would be able to batter down the walls, but the psychological effect would take its toll. Unless we found a way to counter and lessen their advantage. Then an idea grew in my mind.

I kept focused on the men below, and Robard and Maryam rejoined me on the battlement. Robard held two small bundles of arrows.

"You wouldn't believe their pitiful armory," he said. He held up one of the bundles of arrows. "These arrows are for hunting, mostly fowl. They'll not puncture chain mail for certain." As he held them out, I could see they were much shorter than the arrows he used, without iron tips, just a sharpened pointed end. He indicated his own wallet. "I'm nearly out, less than two dozen left, and I have no supplies to make any more. Why don't Franks like the longbow?" he complained.

"I don't know, but what about other weapons? Crossbows?"

"Forty in good working order, and plenty of bolts," he said.

"What about pikes?" I asked.

"No pikes. There are swords and a few throwing axes, but aside from the crossbows, it might as well be empty," Robard mused.

"I don't think they thought about fighting much," Maryam said. "They probably kept enough weapons to keep attackers off the walls, then just waited them out, as Celia said."

I had hoped there would be pikes at least. It could be difficult work turning back the scaling ladders without them.

"We'll have to make do. Robard, get Jean-Luc to station the crossbows on the forward battlement. Maryam, fetch Martine and gather anything that can tip a ladder: rakes, hoes, pitchforks, whatever you can find. Then meet me back here. I have a plan," I said.

Robard and Maryam exchanged a furtive glance, then burst out laughing.

"What's so funny?" I demanded.

"The idea of you with a plan," Maryam teased. "You never have a plan this early. You make everything up as you go along."

"She's got you there, squire," Robard said, still chuckling.

"I most certainly do make plans! There's always a plan. They are just occasionally somewhat *fluid*," I said.

When I told them what I'd thought of, a big smile came to both their faces. They hurried off to their appointed tasks, and I left the battlement to find Celia. I'd need her help in gathering the supplies I required.

If it worked, Sir Hugh was in for a rather large surprise.

fter one hour had passed, Sir Hugh and two knights rode to the gate under a white flag. Sir Hugh asked if we intended to yield. I replied that we did not. Without a word, he turned his horse, and the minute he reached his forward lines, they charged the fortress.

The scaling ladders were in the first wave. Robard had positioned the crossbowmen brilliantly. He broke them into two lines of twenty. The first line fired when the assailants were in range, then stepped back, replaced by the next line, who waited a few seconds and fired another volley while the first line reloaded their bows. It takes nearly a minute for even the most experienced soldier to cock and ready a crossbow, but by concentrating their fire on those carrying the ladders, he slowed their advance. Still, we were vastly outnumbered, and with only forty men shooting, our attackers would eventually gain a foothold on the walls.

Maryam, Celia and Martine led the rest of the villagers on the battlements. Martine and Celia held their swords now, and they ran about, tipping back scaling ladders and shouting encouragement here and there. Maryam wielded a pitchfork as deftly as if it were one of her daggers, pushing back ladder after ladder.

We managed to hold off the first wave, but our men tired, and the time between volleys from the crossbows became longer and longer. Robard kept encouraging them in his own special way.

"Come on, you bloody Franks!" he shouted. "Faster! Faster!" I made a mental note to remind Robard later how he might consider improving his motivational skills.

Robard methodically worked his way through the first bundle of small hunting arrows, shooting quickly but making each missile count. He moved like a dancer among the men at the walls, dodging and darting and seeking out the perfect position for every shot.

While all this happened, I stood below in the courtyard with my "plan," as it were. It was simple, really. I'd constructed three miniature siege engines of my own. Two of Celia's villagers who were handy with tools helped me peg them together from timbers we'd removed from the interior of the castle keep. They weren't fancy, and not likely to be highly accurate, but I didn't need accuracy, only power, for I intended to rain my own version of vengeance down on Sir Hugh.

Each siege engine was primarily a twelve-foot plank mounted on a triangular base and pulled backward by a rope attached to its end. As it bent backward, nearly to the breaking point, the rope was released and the plank shot upward. Each was capable of hurling an object placed on the end of it quite a distance. I had tested one off the back wall of the fortress, out of sight of our attackers, to get a sense of its power. I pried a sizable stone loose from the keep wall and managed to hurl it about sixty yards or so. Perfect.

Now I stood just below the main battlement, in the courtyard behind the gate, waiting for a signal from Robard. With Celia's help, I'd taken several barrels of lard from the kitchen stores. Next to the siege engines, which were spaced below the southwest wall, the lard melted in iron kettles over a fire. We'd taken several earthen jugs, covered them with tinder from the fireboxes and wrapped them with burlap, which we also soaked in the melted fat. Now came the test.

When the next wave of scaling ladders came surging forward, I would release my missiles when they were about fifty yards from the wall. I could hear a yell come up from the lines outside and knew they were on the way. I waited, eager to hear the signal.

"Tristan! Now!" Robard shouted from above.

Each of us manning one of the devices emptied the melted lard into a jug until it was full, and replaced the stopper. It was quickly loaded upon the end of the plank. Then a torch was set to the burlap covering, setting the jug on fire. When the flames burned steadily, two more men pulled back on the rope attached to the planks' end and the boards bent backward.

"Loose!" I shouted and they released the ropes. The boards sprang forward and the flaming jugs flew through the air, clearing the wall by a good ten feet. I only wished I could see what happened next, but I was forced to rely on Robard's report.

He later told me that when the jugs hit the rocky ground outside the fortress walls, they shattered, and the flames came into contact with the melted grease inside. The flaming lard flew in every direction, and with the first shots we managed to set the clothing of dozens of our attackers on fire. I heard screams and horses whinnying, but by then we already had the second round of jugs loaded and ready to fly. I would have only a few minutes before the soldiers recovered and spread out from each other enough to limit the missiles' effects.

"Loose!" The jugs flew, and again I could hear the screams as we found more targets.

We let several more go before Robard signaled us from the battlement. "Hold, Tristan, they're pulling back!"

A cheer went up from the people inside Montségur, and I raced up the ladder to gaze out at the field. Sir Hugh's forces had retreated out of range of the crossbows, and the ground below us was littered with the dead and wounded. Some small pockets of lard still smoldered, and the smoke wafted over the ground.

"Is anyone hurt?" Celia shouted to her people. We had been lucky. We had one man dead at the hand of an attacker who managed to make it over the wall, but Maryam had run him through with her pitchfork. There were a few other villagers with minor wounds, but we had inflicted some serious damage on Sir Hugh's men. Across the field the soldiers milled about, confused and disorganized. Knights, especially Templars, are trained to think victory will easily be theirs. They had found Montségur a much more difficult fruit to pluck.

"Well done, Tristan," Robard said, joining me at the wall. "You gave them something to think about, the jackasses!"

"Yes, I suppose we did," I said. "You did some fancy shooting yourself."

Robard nodded. Maryam and Celia joined us on the battlement, and the four of us peered out at the assembled troops where they had retreated near the tree line.

"What do you think they will do next?" Celia asked.

"I'm not sure," I said, looking across the battlement at Jean-Luc, who would one day make a very capable commander, tending to his injured men and making sure they were resupplied with bolts, food and water. "I think it will be some time until they try another attack. They got more than they bargained for. Sir Hugh is not stupid. He'll come up with something. He will not retreat. Either he will gather more forces, or wait until he starves us out," I said. Something pushed at my leg, and I looked down to find Angel sniffing about. I scratched her ears and she yawned. What would happen to her, I wondered, if Sir Hugh captured the castle?

We had won the first round with a little trickery and the overconfidence of our enemy. They would not be so easily surprised the next time. Celia's faith in her people was palpable, but they could not hold out forever. I had to do something to give them a better chance of survival.

"I know that look!" Robard said as he studied my face. "You have another one of your plans?"

"In fact I do," I said. "We're leaving."

"Leaving? How?" Celia asked with a fair measure of alarm in her face.

"Yes, Templar, how?" Maryam joined in. "You won't be able to get past Sir Hugh or his men. If you were lucky, you might outrace them to the trees and slip away in the forest, but his men will ride you down. The only other way is climbing down the cliffs, and you can't possibly . . ." Maryam stopped when she saw the look on my face.

"No. You can't be serious. Do you think . . . No." She couldn't get the words out. "Robard, tell him. Tell him he can't do what he's thinking."

"I'd be happy to, but I have no idea what he's thinking," Robard replied, confused.

"He wants to climb down the cliffs," Celia said. "And he's a fool, for it can't be done."

"Celia, you don't understand. He won't give up. He will stay here until you surrender or he will gather enough regimentos to overwhelm you. You have your people to think about. I have to go. It's the only way." I tried to make her understand. I had no desire to leave, just when I had found her again. But I could not let her or her people suffer further on my account.

"Tristan, they might be right," Robard cut in. "If you want to leave, fine, but wouldn't it be better to try slipping through the woods at nightfall?"

"I've thought of that. It's too risky. Sir Hugh will have his men covering the woods around the clock. We have no horses, and we're no match on foot against well-mounted Templars, even in a thick forest."

"I'd rather take my chances against the knights than fall to my death," Robard said with a shiver.

"I don't expect any of you to join me. You can stay here. When Sir Hugh finds out I'm gone, he'll leave to come after me. You'll be safe," I promised.

Robard and Maryam looked at each other. Then at me.

"What?" I asked.

"Why are you doing this, Tristan? Why are you risking your life like this?" Maryam demanded. Robard nodded in agreement.

I decided they needed to know. Despite what Sir Thomas had told me, they deserved the truth. They were not power-mad Templars or treasure seekers or wanting to control the world. They were born to simple lives. Now they were warriors who wanted nothing more than to return to their homes, but they had given up much to help me. Both of them had saved my life numerous times. And Celia as well. They were my friends.

"I will tell you everything . . . I promise—" I was interrupted by a shout from Jean-Luc. Sir Hugh was riding back toward the fortress, holding a white flag aloft.

My confession would have to wait.

# 20

ir Hugh had two other knights with him. This time, I kept Robard on the battlement, his long-bow at the ready. Jean-Luc and two of the cross-bowmen joined me, leaving Maryam and Celia inside. Before I left, and for the first time in the past many weeks, I removed the satchel from my shoulder. Handing it to Maryam, I said, "Promise me this: if anything happens to me, see to it this satchel finds its way to Father William of the Church of the Holy Redeemer in Rosslyn, Scotland."

Maryam's eyes narrowed. "I thought you said you needed to take testimony to the Master of the Order in London."

"I'll explain later," I said. With the Frenchmen behind me we slipped through the gate and walked across the rocky ground to where Sir Hugh squirmed nervously astride a speckled gray warhorse.

"Are you a woman?" he asked when I stood in front of him and his two companions.

"I beg your pardon?"

"Is this how Sir Thomas trained his squires? To fight like women, with fire and trickery? What's wrong, squire? Are you and your peas-ants incapable of fighting like men?" he yelled.

"If you find you've lost your taste for battle, feel free to leave the field," I replied calmly.

"You kill my men with flaming grease, squire? Are you a warrior or a cook?" he thundered as he spurred his horse forward, his hand going to the hilt of his sword as if he meant to draw it and strike me down. In an instant Jean-Luc and his men raised their crossbows and pointed them directly at him.

"Not another step, Sir Hugh," I warned. "These men will kill you where you stand. You can't win here. Withdraw. You have no chance. We can survive for months inside this fortress. We have plenty of food and water. There is no shortage of weapons."

"I will have it, squire. I will have it! Do you hear me?" Sir Hugh reined his horse backward, in line with the other knights. Jean Luc's men slowly lowered their crossbows, but Jean-Luc, apparently a good judge of character, kept his pointed at Sir Hugh's chest.

"Mark this, squire. Your life is forfeit. I will see you and everyone in Montségur dead. You will give me what I want or I will not stop until everyone inside your fortress is nothing but a pile of bones. I don't care how long it takes. Do you understand me?"

"Sir Hugh, I'm tired of this. And tired of you and your empty threats," I replied wearily. "Take my advice and withdraw from this place. If you try to take this fortress, we will make you pay and pay and pay again. We will not yield. With my last breath I will destroy what you seek before you lay eyes on it. Do you understand me?"

Sir Hugh's face became a vision of anguish and frustration. The very thing he wanted more than anything in the world was within his reach, yet unattainable. He pursed his lips, and even over the distance between us and the noise of the wind, I could hear his breath coming hard and fast in tortured gasps. His gloved hands were knotted on the reins of his horse as if he might wring water from them. In contrast, the two knights with him sat atop their mounts as still as stones.

"However, in the interest of preventing further bloodshed, I will make you a deal, Sir Hugh," I said.

He looked at me, his eyes hooded, but with just a glint of expectancy within them. He said nothing, waiting for me to speak.

"Leave the field, take your regimento and retire to the small hamlet that lies at the entrance of this valley. You must have passed through it on your way here. There is a small inn there. You leave this mountain and promise never to return, and in three days' time I will meet you there and give you what you seek."

Sir Hugh waved his hand at me and smirked.

"You must think me a fool, squire. The minute I withdraw, you vanish into the forest. No, I think not."

"Where would I go?" I said, pointing to the mountains surrounding us. "We are on top of a mountain. The cliffs and peaks around us make the way north impossible. The only way out is through the valley below. With you and your men stationed there, it would be impossible for me to slip past."

"No," he said.

"Then I suggest you send your men against the walls again. Many more of them will die. How long do you think they'll be willing to wait here?" I asked. "And how long do you think the High Counsel and his troops will remain here? You two appeared to be on poor terms."

"They will remain here until I command them otherwise!" he spat. I shrugged, dismissing his outburst. Something was off about his response, and looking past him at the assembled forces, I figured it out. The High Counsel's men were not in evidence. All I saw were Templar banners and tunics. There were none of the green-and-white markings of Father Renard's men, and I wondered if he had slipped away or retreated.

"Is that right?" I asked him. "It would appear you have lost some of your forces. What happened? Did the High Counsel decide you were no longer friends?"

Sir Hugh waved his hand in the air dismissively, as if the whereabouts of the High Counsel were of no concern to him. I tried to keep him off balance.

"And your Templar comrades? Do you think they will tolerate such losses? If they were of your own regimento, maybe, but I'm sure you haven't shared your reasons for being here with them. How long do you think it will be before they grow weary of your tactics?" In the eyes of one of the men behind Sir Hugh I caught something: fear mixed with hesitation. It told me that the moment might be closer than even Sir Hugh thought. If anything, he had repeatedly proven incapable of leading men in battle. His troops would quickly grow to resent him.

Sir Hugh raised and lowered himself in the stirrups of his saddle, a bundle of nervous energy. For several seconds he said nothing. Then a smile came to his face.

"Very well, squire. I accept your terms. We will withdraw and wait for you in the hamlet at the head of the valley. You have until noon three days hence to show up with the . . . to show yourself there. If you are not there by noon, my regimento will put every one of the villagers in that hamlet to the sword. All of them, men, women and children, do you understand? They all die. Tell your princess those are my terms. See how far her hospitality extends then, squire. I will kill them all. *Comprenez-vous?*" he added for the benefit of Jean-Luc and his men-at-arms.

My heart sank, for I had made a terrible mistake, one I had no idea how to correct. I had hoped he would agree and I could escape down the mountain. But he had nearly struck down the High Counsel, and now his madness was overtaking him and he would kill everyone in his path if he thought it necessary. I tried to keep my face a mask, but wasn't sure I did. Our first step was to free Celia and her people from Montségur.

"I'll be there, Sir Hugh," I said. "In three days."

"If you are not, then those people will die. Count on it." Sir Hugh whipped his horse, riding back to the lines. One of the knights hesitated before following.

"Brother! Wait!" I called after him, but he did not stop, only turned to give me a brief glance.

We began the short trek back toward the castle. Jean-Luc walked beside me, his two men keeping an eye on the retreating knights.

"What you do now, *Anglais?*" he asked in his best English. I could tell from his tone that he knew what was happening and was worried, and I couldn't blame him. He understood enough to know what Sir Hugh had said.

"I don't know, Jean-Luc," I said. "I must talk to Celia."

Robard, Maryam and Celia had clustered around us, and Angel strolled up and sat on her haunches, staring at me.

"What did that pile of polecat dung have to say for himself?" Robard asked.

"I made a deal. He will quit the siege and meet me in the small village at the head of the valley in three days. You and your people will be free to go, Celia," I said.

"What? No, you can't do it! He'll kill you!" Maryam cried.

"I don't have a choice," I said.

"Why not?" Celia asked, the tone in her voice saying she more than agreed with Maryam.

"You should have just let me shoot him," Robard said.

Celia hushed him.

"Explain yourself, Templar," she said.

"I . . . made . . . a mistake . . . a miscalculation. I was so intent on getting Sir Hugh away from here and your people, I forgot who I was dealing with. He'll withdraw and wait for us in the village, all right, but if I don't show up, he's threatened to kill everyone in the village. Even the women and children."

"I see," said Celia quietly. She put her hands on her hips and bowed her head, staring at the ground, lost in thought.

"I'm so sorry, Celia. I won't let any harm come to those innocent—"

Celia paid no attention and called sharply for Jean-Luc. When he appeared, she spoke to him quickly and he darted off.

"Come with me, all of you," she said.

We climbed back up to the battlement above the main gate and surveyed the ground. Sir Hugh and the regimento of Templars were retreating just as he had promised. They had carried little equipment, and those who weren't already mounted were in the process of saddling their horses and moving out. Indeed, a line of them were already heading onto the trail and back down the mountain into the forest, toward the village.

Jean-Luc returned shortly with another one of the villagers, who carried a long horn made of brass. He put the horn to his lips and sounded several long, low notes through it. The sound echoed off the surrounding mountains.

"What is this? What are you doing?" I asked her.

She laughed. "Your Sir Hugh is in for a rude surprise. It is a signal to the people of the valley, those who were not able to come to Montségur and instead hid out on their farms and in the forest."

"Most every place we passed through on the way here was deserted," said Robard.

Celia nodded. "Yes, since we have become enemies of the church, we needed a way to sound the alarm when those who might do us harm draw near. It was Philippe's idea, actually. This horn has just warned everyone that trouble is coming. The message will be delivered up and down the valley. Sir Hugh will find no one in the village to murder."

I laughed at the ingenuity of it. I could almost see the smile on Philippe's face, knowing his clever method had outwitted Sir Hugh.

"Are you positive it will work?" I wasn't sure.

"Certain," she replied.

"Then I guess this settles it," I said, gazing out at the mountains to the north.

"Settles what?" Maryam asked.

I looked at the faces of all my friends.

"I leave at first light."

# 21

e had moved to an empty chamber room inside the keep. There was much I needed to tell my friends, and I didn't wish to be overheard. As always, Angel trotted along with us. Maryam still held the satchel tightly in her hands. She made no move to return it to me yet. In fact, she looked as if she would be more than happy to smack me with it. I smiled at her, but she frowned back, not in the mood for charm.

"I don't understand," Robard said. "If Sir Hugh is gone, why don't we take to the woods and leave?"

"He'll be watching. And suppose Celia's warning doesn't reach everyone? He'll kill them. I cannot live with the risk. I need to go," I said, removing the battle sword from my back and unhooking my belt, relieved to be free of the weapons. It was good to not be weighed down by all those things. At St. Alban's I never carried more than the shirt on my back and a hoe. Since leaving I was continuously weighted down by more things. The swords, the Grail, they all symbolized my obligations and my duty.

"I still think you're crazy," Maryam huffed.

"Maybe I am." I shrugged.

Twilight approached, and the interior of the keep was lit by torchlight and oil lamps. Now the time had come to tell my friends the truth, but I found the words stuck in my throat. In my mind's eye, the face of Sir Thomas implored me to keep the secret of what I carried, not only because it would make the Grail safer, but because it would be an unfair burden to put upon my friends. He didn't take lightly this duty he had given me. He trusted me to do the right thing. Now the right thing was to tell my friends for what they had risked their lives, and in Celia's case, the lives of her people.

"I don't carry dispatches or testimony for the Master of the Order," I told them.

Maryam and Robard looked at each other.

"No surprise—we already guessed it had to be something more important," Maryam said.

It was hard to say it. Though the moment was here, I couldn't help but feel I was still disappointing Sir Thomas. It was easier just to show them.

With trembling hands I opened the satchel. Removing all of my other gear, I flipped open the secret compartment and pulled out the Grail. I removed the linen covering, holding it out so they could see it. No one said anything, because they were unsure of exactly what I was showing them.

"You risked our lives for a vase?" Robard finally asked.

"It's not a vase, Robard." I set it on the table next to the satchel.

"It looks like one," he replied.

"Tristan, what is it? Why is it so important?" Celia asked.

"It's the Holy Grail," I answered.

Robard burst out laughing, but Maryam's and Celia's faces

turned to stone. Both of them studied the Grail intently while Robard continued to laugh.

"You're joking, right?" he finally asked when he had composed himself.

"No."

"Well, the only problem is the Grail doesn't exist, so you *are* carrying a vase." He laughed again, finding the whole idea amusing.

"Robard, it is *not* a vase. Sir Thomas gave it to me with strict instructions on its care. He wouldn't have sent me into this much danger unless it was really important," I insisted.

"Not even to save your life? You were facing certain death if you remained in Acre—you said so yourself. What if he just wanted to get you to safety, so he concocted a story to remove you from peril?" he suggested.

"I . . . No . . . He did not *concoct* anything! This is *the* Holy Grail. *The Cup of Christ!* I've seen it do things with my own eyes!" I don't know why I was so frustrated. Why should Robard believe me? If I were in his position, I wouldn't believe me either. He helps rescue someone from bandits who just *happens* to be carrying the most sacred relic known to man? No wonder he was laughing.

"What can I do to convince you it's true?" I asked.

"I don't know. Wait. I've got it! Why don't you have it perform a miracle?" he joked.

"It already has," I replied.

"When?"

"When you shot me in Outremer, the Grail stayed your arrow." I fingered the still visible hole in the satchel. "The arrow entered here, right where I carried it. It should have shattered, but it didn't even leave a scratch."

"Hold! You shot him too?" Maryam asked, a look of horror on her face.

"Yes. No. I mean, yes, I shot him, but it was an accident. I was trying to shoot you," Robard stammered.

"What?!" Maryam nearly shouted. "But I don't understand. You shot me when we attacked the two of you outside of Tyre. I was wounded and defenseless after that. Are you saying that you tried to shoot me again?"

"It's not . . . I mean . . . He got in the way . . . I didn't know you . . . Things were different then!" Robard said.

"I was lying helpless on the ground and you were going to shoot me?" she went on.

"It's not like that! How was I to know you weren't still dangeous? You had daggers and had already tried to kill us once! Besides, Tristan got in the way and . . ."

"Enough!" I barked at them. "We don't have time for this. This is the Holy Grail. Sir Thomas told me it was, and I trust him. Besides, I've seen it do other things, things that can't be explained."

Maryam and Robard stopped abruptly and both glanced at me. Celia, who had been silent during the exchange, looked at me, then down at the floor, as if she were trying to decide something very important.

"What things?" Robard said, his eyebrows knitted in disbelief.

"It's hard to explain."

"Try." Robard was resolute.

"Sometimes . . . it makes a noise when I am . . . when we are in danger," I said.

"What kind of noise?" he scoffed.

Celia and Maryam both spoke at once.

"A low humming sound," they said softly. Their voices were so quiet, they were barely heard.

Robard's head snapped around to look at them, and now it was my turn to stare in disbelief. If Maryam had heard it, why hadn't she said anything? Celia had mentioned it when she found me on the beach, but I'd ignored her and changed the subject.

"I've heard the sound," Maryam said. "The first time was on the night when we attacked your camp. I had no idea what it was or what it meant. When I heard it, it was I who led my fellow Hashshashin to your camp, not my leader. It was almost like the sound drew me there. I told myself it was Allah's voice carrying me to my hidden enemies."

Maryam was pacing now. She looked at the Grail. "Then when you survived the attack and nursed me back to health, I heard it in the underbrush as the Saracens searched for us. But I had no idea it was this holy object. All this time I thought it was you."

"Maybe it is him," Celia spoke up.

"What? What do you mean? What's so special about an orphaned squire to a Templar Knight?" Robard asked, clearly not believing or understanding anything we were saying.

"What is so special about a squire, you ask? Wasn't a simple carpenter from Nazareth chosen by your God for greatness? And wasn't a common merchant chosen by God to lead Maryam's people? Look at who was given this duty: someone who is kind and good and loyal, and puts the lives of others above his own. Why Tristan? Why *not* Tristan?" Celia said, never taking her eyes away from mine.

I felt the heat rise to my face. Try as I might, I could not keep my chest from swelling. The sounds of the world stopped and everything was quiet. Maryam and Robard and even Angel melted away, and for a moment it was only the two of us. She thought this of me? Would I ever be able to live up to her?

"I heard the same sound Maryam describes as we rode along the beach," she went on. "When I asked Tristan if he'd heard it as well, he changed the subject. He knew what I was talking about—I could see it in his eyes. He didn't want to tell me, and now I understand why. I think it was the Grail leading me to him. We Cathars do not believe the way your church does, Tristan. We do not believe in things like divinity or saints or miracles. And yet I heard this sound. And so did Maryam. So I must pray for understanding, because it seems clear you are carrying a miracle."

"What? I'm not much for church, God knows, but even I know blasphemy when I hear it! God would never allow something so sacred to be used in such a frivolous manner," Robard said. "Assuming this is the Holy Grail, which it's not! I've been with Tristan the whole time and I haven't heard anything. Nothing at all! I don't believe there even *is* a Holy Grail."

"There is." I shrugged. There was no way to easily convince Robard. "This is it."

"So what do we do now?" Maryam asked.

"I have to do my duty. Sir Thomas ordered me to get to Scotland and make sure it is safe," I said.

"I understand," said Celia. "And I would go with you if I could. But I have a responsibility to my people."

"Yes, I know," I said, surprised at how much the news disappointed me. I knew she couldn't go, but still wanted her to. What was wrong with me?

"I'm with you," Maryam said. "I will do all I can to help you finish this. I will help you keep the prophet's cup safe."

I smiled my thanks at her and looked at Robard.

"What?" he asked, surprised. "Did I not tell you earlier I was in this to the end? Nothing has changed. I still don't believe it. But I knew you just weren't carrying papers. I thought maybe you'd stolen something, like gold, and was going to tell you to just give it back, whatever it was. Then we met Sir Hugh, and I realized that whatever you had of his, he probably didn't deserve it anyway. But I didn't think you thought you were carrying a priceless relic. I still don't. It looks like a vase to me!"

Despite myself I couldn't help laughing, and for the briefest instant I wondered what I had ever done to deserve friends like these. I was no longer angry with Sir Thomas for the burden he'd given me, for without it I would never have met these three. That could not be measured.

"There is something else I need to tell you," I said.

Robard looked at Maryam. "You realize he's probably going to tell us his tunic is made from the Virgin Mother's veil or something."

"Robard!" Maryam said, shocked at his blasphemy.

"What?" He threw up his arms and shrugged, feigning innocence.

"That's not it. I carry only one relic. As far as I know. The way my luck is going, Sir Thomas' battle sword could belong to King Arthur. But there is something else you should know." And I told them all about my encounters with King Richard and his guards. Every detail. I wanted to cleanse my soul of all my secrets, and once I got going, I couldn't stop.

Robard pursed his lips. "If I didn't know better"—he stopped and walked to the window and spat—"I would think the Lionheart wants you dead."

"I know," I said.

"But why?" Maryam nearly shouted. "What interest could he possibly have in you?"

I shrugged, for I had no answer. "I just wanted you all to know everything. Before our next step. If you want out, I understand."

Robard and Maryam didn't hesitate. "We're in," he said. "I don't expect to have to have this conversation again." He clapped me on the shoulder. Maryam and Celia smiled.

Angel gave a happy yip, which a moment later became a low growl. Stopping to listen, we heard the rising shouts of alarm and general commotion coming from outside. Just then Jean-Luc knocked at the doorway and threw the door open. He spoke quickly to Celia, then rushed away.

"What is the matter?" I asked.

"Your friend Sir Hugh has returned," she said, "with more men this time. His leaving was a ruse. We are under attack!"

e ran out of the keep and across the bailey. Jean-Luc had moved quickly to man the forward battlement. Other villagers were running about, bringing their pitchforks and swords forward, determined to drive back Sir Hugh and his invading hordes.

"Start the fires!" I yelled. My siege engines still stood at the ready. I hoped we would have enough earthen jugs and time to use them before Sir Hugh's men could get a foothold on the walls.

"Tristan," Robard yelled as we ran toward the battlements, "I don't have enough arrows to even slow them down. You had better come up with something quick."

"Can you shoot a crossbow?" I asked.

"Of course I can shoot a crossbow, but why would I want to?" he scoffed.

"Because it's all we have at the moment. Save what arrows you have for when they are really needed."

Robard nodded and cut toward the armory. Maryam and Celia were rallying the villagers along the northwest wall. Several of the village elders, with Angel's assistance, were herding the children back into the keep. They would be safe there.

While they stoked the fires, I raced up the ladder to the forward battlement to survey the field. I was shocked by what lay before me. A quick count of regimento flags told me there were more than six hundred Templars on the field before us. Even with the loss of the High Counsel's men, wherever they had gone, Sir Hugh had still gained numbers. For a moment, I was glad to at least be rid of Father Renard, though the way my luck went I was sure I would encounter him again somewhere. Sir Hugh was more than enough to deal with at the moment. If he had managed to gather more Templars from nearby commanderies, would more be arriving? And how soon?

It was almost dark but still light enough to see the lines forming. Several small groups had already raced forward to the walls and were making a halfhearted attempt to use scaling ladders, but they were paying a dreadful price as Jean-Luc's crossbowmen cut through them.

At first I was confused by their tactics. Why were they not more deliberate in trying to overcome us on the battlements? I could not see Sir Hugh on the field in the gathering darkness, but something wasn't right here. The Templars at the walls shouted now and then, and a few of them even chucked a few rocks at the crossbowmen, ducking behind shields when the bowmen answered with a shot, but their surge was unorganized and lacked intensity.

Then Sir Hugh's plan was revealed and my mouth fell open to my chest.

From out of the tree line, pulled by several teams of horses and dozens of men, came a giant battering ram. It moved on four huge wooden wheels supported by a triangular base. From the framework hung a log, carved by ax to a sharp point, covered with an iron casing. It would be rolled up to the gate and then several teams of men would swing the log back and forth until the metal-tipped point battered down the doors.

Wooden shielding had been affixed over the frame to repel our flaming missiles and crossbowmen from harming the men below it. And I was sure the wood was green and coated in mud so it wouldn't catch fire easily, at least not before they had broken through the gates.

As I watched the attack unfold, I was angry at myself for allowing Sir Hugh to dupe me so easily. I should have known he would never agree to leave without a fight. He had only sought to buy time until his reinforcements arrived and he could attack in force. But as Sir Thomas once told me, battle is no time to dwell on one's mistakes. I had to regain my focus and figure a way to counter this move.

Down below, next to my small siege engines, the kettles of lard over the fires were bubbling. Robard, Jean-Luc and the crossbowmen held the battlement and pushed back the scaling ladders, but the men-at-arms below were not at all interested in climbing the ladders; they were only buying time and making us waste precious bolts until the battering ram could be rolled into place.

"Jean-Luc!" I shouted. "Hold your fire! Save your bolts for the men pushing the battering ram!" Celia stood at the southwest corner shouting orders.

"Celia, come with me, please. Hurry!" She left Martine in charge and we made our way down to the courtyard.

We reached the fires below a few seconds later. "I need you to tell everyone manning a siege engine to get the lard as hot as possible and hoist those kettles up on the parapet over the main gate.

We'll need ropes and timbers! Get them to hurry!" Frantic shouting came from the battlement above us, and there was more noise outside as the battering ram slowly made its way toward the gate.

Celia repeated my orders to her men, and they went about their tasks diligently and in a hurry. More firewood was carried from the bailey, and the fires beneath the kettles were stoked again. Several men ran forward carrying timbers on their backs and shoulders that they handed up to those manning the battlement. In short order they had lashed together a small windlass that would work perfectly for our needs.

"Robard! How much farther until they reach the gate?" I shouted up to him.

"Not far! One hundred paces, I'd say. If you have something in mind, you better be quick!"

Everything was in place. I grabbed the rope hanging from the windlass and tied it carefully about the handle of the big iron kettle. When it was secure, the men above us hoisted the kettle slowly upward toward the battlement. One of the villagers on the ground held a long pole that he kept locked against the side of the kettle to keep it from tipping.

"Hurry!" Maryam shouted from her spot on the wall. "They're almost here!"

The kettle rose a few more feet, and then we all heard and felt a thundering boom against the main gate. The noise was deafening and the walls shook, but the door held. A few seconds later another boom sounded against the door. We were almost in place now as the men above moved the kettle onto the battlement. A small pile of torches had been brought out of the keep, and grabbing one, I laid it to the flame in the fire. When it caught, I raced up the ladder. Running forward, I peered over the wall and saw the ram right beneath us.

The ram thundered against the door again. The door still held. Shouting out orders to the men, we lifted the kettle onto the top of the wall right above the main gate.

"Wait until they roll it forward again!" I shouted over the din.

Down below, we watched as the men pushing the ram backed up, then came forward slowly, then came faster as they strained toward the door. When the iron point was a few feet from the door, I gave the command: "Loose!" I shouted, and the kettle was tipped forward and the hot grease went splashing down on the ram. Some of it splashed over the wooden shielding and onto the men nearby, who screamed and ran away. Carefully measuring the distance, I tossed the torch, which landed on the topmost wooden shield.

At first nothing happened. Then with a loud whoosh, the grease caught and the forward-most part of the ram burst into flames. Several of the men hiding under the shielding lost their nerve at the sight of the fire and ran from their cover.

"Now!" shouted Robard, and the crossbowmen mowed the running men down like wheat before a scythe. Their screams and cries rose up to us in the darkness.

"Get the next kettle ready!" I shouted. "They'll regroup and the ram will be back!"

As I feared, the wood on the shield covering the battering ram had been coated in mud. As the flames died, I could hear orders being shouted and see men moving toward the ram as it was reinforced.

The attacks came on through the night, but we managed to hold them off until daybreak. The ram was burned and scorched but still operable, and Celia had informed me we'd soon run out of barrels of lard. As the sun poked over the horizon, the fighting halted as the men on the field rested before their next assault.

The four of us met on the wall to take stock of the situation. Far off, near the tree line, I could see Sir Hugh on horseback, watching and directing the activity on the field.

"He won't give up as long as I'm here," I said.

My friends said nothing.

"Celia, can you spare us some ropes?" She didn't look at me for a long time, but simply stared out at the forces arrayed against her. Finally she nodded.

"Oh no. Tristan, I saved you from bandits, you went through a shipwreck and a siege, and now you have a wish to plummet to your death? No wonder the monks who raised you only let you work the garden! If you'd done anything else, I'm sure you would have found a thousand ways to injure yourself and others!" Robard blurted.

I ignored Robard's jibe. "I think it's time for us to leave," I said.

# 23

ight from the east fluttered into the valley surrounding us. The Templars outside the gates were now silent, but I knew another attack would commence before long. I stood at the rear wall of Montségur with Maryam, Celia and Robard. Angel moved nervously around my feet. Staring down the sheer rock wall, my stomach tightened and I wanted to reconsider my plan. But I couldn't waver. I looked at the crossbowmen on the battlement opposite where we stood. They all sat slumped with their backs to the wall, resting and waiting to fight again. Sir Hugh would starve us out if necessary. I needed to get him to chase me instead so Celia's people could return to their homes. But then, as I stood looking down the cliff face, my head swimming, I thought that a few more weeks bottled up inside a fortress might not be so bad.

"Tristan, are you sure this is the only way?" Celia asked.

"Yes," I said quietly.

"Ha!" said Robard to no one in particular. For approximately the twelfth time, he was checking and rechecking the rope we had looped around a parapet and lowered over the side.

"Of course he's sure," Maryam chimed in. "He has a *plan*."

Maryam was not in love with the idea of climbing down the side of the mountain by rope either.

It was easy to ignore barbs, busy as I was trying to memorize Celia's face. Her eyes were tired, but they still drew me in. I hated to leave Montségur. To leave her.

Taking her hand, I gave her a small piece of parchment. With ink and quill I had found inside the keep, I had written a brief note to Sir Hugh.

"If you can withstand another assault to buy us some time, I would be grateful," I said fearfully, worried at the cost her people would pay to give us a head start. "Then I would have you ask to speak to Sir Hugh under a flag of truce. Don't venture outside until his forces withdraw from the wall, and make sure you meet him in range of the crossbows. Jean-Luc will know what to do. Give Sir Hugh this note and tell him I'm gone. Tell him you'll allow two of his men, but not him, to search the castle to confirm it. When he realizes we're already gone, he should be itching to get away from here and come after us."

Celia nodded, taking the note from me and secreting it in her tunic.

"What does the note say?" Robard asked.

"Nothing much. I just told him farewell, leave these good folk alone, and he'll never catch me," I said.

"That should work," Maryam said.

"Good note. I need to learn how to write one of these days," Robard commented as he pulled again and again at the rope.

Martine joined us on the wall now to say her good-byes as well.

"Good-bye, Martine," I said. "Please take care of her."

*"Oui, monsieur,"* she said. Her eyes filled with tears, but she willed them away. I hadn't gotten to know her well, but I had witnessed her fierce loyalty to Celia. Like Philippe, I believed Martine would gladly give her life for Celia.

"One more thing," I said. "Would you mind looking after Angel?" I pointed to her, and as soon as I did, she snarled and jumped up, putting her forepaws on my hip.

"I would, but I think she prefers to go with you," Celia said.

"I don't see how we can take her!" I said.

She dug at my hip with her paws. "Quiet, girl!" I said. But my words had no effect.

"I don't see how we can leave her," Robard said.

"What? Why not?" I replied.

"Because she doesn't want to stay," Maryam said.

Martine took action. She removed the cape she wore over her tunic and scooped Angel up into her arms. Very quickly she twisted the cape around and around, tying several knots, and before I knew it, she looped it over my head and shoulders. Angel wiggled against my chest and poked her head out of the covering.

Everyone laughed. I couldn't help but chuckle myself. If she was so determined, I would have no choice but to bring her along.

"Now you carry your dog like a Cathar woman carries her baby," Celia said.

Despite the fact that we were likely to plunge to our deaths in a few moments, Robard and Maryam found this extremely funny.

"Could you make one of those carriers for me?" Robard asked Martine. She didn't understand him, so she just nodded. "Never mind," he said glumly.

The time had come to leave and yet, looking at Celia, I found myself rooted to the spot. My body was unwilling to move, yet I knew I had to go. The morning light had painted the world a mellow gold, and despite the dust and sweat that clung to Celia, she was still beautiful and I wished more than anything to change my mind.

"Celia . . . I . . ." There was nothing left to say. My silence was physically painful, as though the seconds would never pass, but almost in slow motion she stepped forward and threw her arms around me. I went as still as a statue, not sure if I could, or should, return her embrace.

She stepped back from me and I could see the slightest tear at the corner of her eye. "Good-bye, Tristan. Robard. Maryam. My people will not forget you. We will remember what you have done for us. If it hadn't been for all of you, the High Counsel would have caught us before we reached Montségur. And you helped us drive him away. Do not worry about Sir Hugh. I believe you. When he learns you are gone, he will lose all interest in us. "

Robard and Maryam said nothing, too humbled and embarrassed to reply. They merely nodded repeatedly until Maryam finally hugged Celia.

"Good-bye, Celia," Maryam whispered. "I'm so sorry about what happened when we first met. I hope you'll forgive me."

"Don't take it personally, Celia," Robard chimed in. "She usually tries to kill all of her friends first."

Celia laughed as she hugged Robard. I still couldn't move until Maryam nudged me and whispered that it was time to go. Reluctantly, I stepped up onto the parapet and looked again over the side. Celia had called a few men from their posts to lower us by rope to the ground beneath the northeast wall. Facing away from Sir Hugh's forces attacking from the opposite side, we could pick our way down the cliff and, I hoped, make it to the valley below.

I would go first. Gripping the rope in my hand, I sat down on the parapet with my legs dangling over the wall. One of Celia's carpenters had fashioned another windlass, which would give us stability as we were lowered. The men took up the rope, and I looped it over and around my shoulders, being careful not to hurt the dog. She wiggled a little bit more inside her carrier and then stilled. In fact she might have even gone to sleep.

Maryam had taken the battle sword from me and carried it across her back. Robard had his bow and remaining arrows in his wallet. He also carried a pouch of food Celia's cooks had prepared for us. We all carried water skins, and Robard and Maryam each held a coil of the longest rope the Cathars could spare.

I took a breath, offered up a silent prayer, and nodded to the men working the rope. Gently I let myself go over the side. My last glimpse of Celia was of her ice-blue eyes watching me disappear from sight.

"I promise, Templar," I heard her say. "We will remember this."

A few seconds later I stood on the small ledge at the bottom of the fortress. Completely removed from the safety of the walls of Montségur.

# 24

s I stood at the base of the wall, waiting for Robard and Maryam to join me, I reflected on all I had learned since I had left St. Alban's. Templar laws. Sword fighting and battle tactics. I don't like ships. Hashshashin are not all bad once you get to know them. These were just a few bits of the knowledge now crowding about for space inside my brain. But along with the many new things I'd seen and done since I'd given up my sheltered existence, I had a revelation and it was this: climbing down a nearly vertical cliff is even harder than it looks.

We had about three feet of space at the bottom of the wall before the rocky ground broke off and plunged nearly straight down. The rope that had lowered us was untied from the windlass and dropped to me. We now had three lengths of rope, but even tied together they would not reach the bottom of the cliff.

"Madness," Robard muttered under his breath, standing with his back planted firmly against the castle wall. His eyes were closed and his fists were clenched.

"What do you think, Tristan?" Maryam asked. "Tie the ropes together, or go in sections and tie off as we go?"

I was busy at the time, staring at the sheer wall and imagining what the impact of my body at the bottom would feel and sound like. Would Tristan and Maryam be able to hear it up above or would the sound of my death be carried away on the wind?

"What?" I answered.

"Templar, you got us into this!" Maryam shouted, suddenly angry. "Now wake up, pay attention and get us out of it!" She smacked me on the shoulder for emphasis.

"Madness," Robard repeated.

"All right," I said. "I think the best approach would be for you both to hold the rope while I climb down as far as I can. I'll find a place to tie it off, then Maryam, you come next." A small boulder stuck up out of the ground at my feet. Testing it with my foot, it proved sturdy.

"This will work. Robard, once Maryam is down with me, lower your rope down and we'll tie it to hers. You can pull it back up, and then lower yourself down to us by using this rock like a windlass. We'll be able to hold on to you all the way down. With any luck, we can repeat this method all the way down the mountain. It will be easy, actually," I claimed. In reality it wouldn't be easy at all, but Robard's eyes were growing wider by the minute, and I wanted to get us moving before he became too frozen to move.

"Madness," Robard said again.

Luckily the side of the cliff was rough and uneven, giving me numerous foot- and handholds. It took me several minutes to climb down even a small way, but after a while I found a rhythm. Then God chose to smite me again, for the angle of the cliff became steeper and I found myself hugging the rock wall, unable to move down or to the side.

"Maryam, Robard! I'm stuck!" I hollered up at them.

"What do you mean, *stuck*?" Robard shouted back.

"How many different meanings of *stuck* are there? I can't move!"

There were no handholds nearby that I could see. My feet were wedged against the cliff and I held on to the rope with both hands, but my feet and legs trembled.

Maryam peered down at me. "Do you want us to pull you back up?" she shouted.

"No! Do you see anyplace where I might be able find a foothold?"

Maryam was silent while she studied the surface around me.

"Hurry up and do something!" Robard shouted at Maryam. "He's getting heavy!"

"Tristan, about ten feet below you on your right I can see an outcropping. You should be able to reach it. You'll have to push out and swing over to it," she yelled.

"What? Push out and swing? I'm barely hanging on as it is!" Push out and swing indeed! Even though Maryam and Robard held most of my weight, my legs and arms were losing strength.

"I didn't know Templars frightened so easily. You are tied off and we *are* holding on to the rope, after all," she shouted down to me.

"Maryam!"

"Relax. Trust me. You can do it. Push out and to your right, then we'll let you down about ten feet. It's right there. You'll see!" She tried to sound encouraging. It didn't matter, though, because I definitely could not stay where I was.

Gently, I pushed out with my legs and tried to swing to my right. But I stumbled against the wall and tried to scrabble back into position with my feet. I couldn't regain my footing and slammed my shoulder against the rock, grimacing as it went numb.

"Ow!" I shouted.

Grabbing the rope as tightly as I could, I pushed back from the cliff face. My momentum swung me out into space. Robard let out more rope and I dropped another five or six feet. As I swung back toward the wall, I thrust outward with my legs to keep from smashing into it.

"You're right over it!" Maryam shouted. "You should be able to reach it with your feet."

Feeling around with my foot, I found the outcropping of rock. It felt solid, with enough room for me to stand. My legs and arms shook from the strain, and I was glad the rope was tied securely around me or I would surely have tumbled the remaining way down.

Below me, another rock ledge jutted out from the side of the cliff. It looked wide enough for Maryam and I to stand on. There was also a small bush there, jutting out from the side of the mountain. I could tie the end of her rope to it as an anchor in case she slipped on the way down.

From up above, the sounds of shouts and cries came from Montségur. Sir Hugh was attacking again. The longer we delayed, the dearer the price to those in the fortress.

"Robard! I need about six feet of slack!" I shouted up to him. He complied, and I grasped the rope and pushed off with my legs, scrabbling downward. I managed to make it to the ledge in a few seconds.

"I've found a good spot!" I shouted up to Robard and Maryam. "Maryam, you come down next and then we'll help Robard!"

Robard released his grip on my rope and dropped it down to me. Wrapping it securely around the bush, I gave myself enough slack to move about on the ledge but not enough to fall.

Whereas I had struggled like a fish tossed up on the shore, Maryam took to the mountainside like a goat. It must have come from growing up in the desert with lots of rocks nearby. With the rope lashed around her waist she attacked the cliff fearlessly, and, in less than ten minutes, had made her way down the cliff to stand shoulder-to-shoulder with me on the small ledge.

"Roomy," she said sarcastically.

"Isn't it, though?" I said. "We're ready, Robard!" I shouted up to him.

We waited, but Robard didn't say anything back. And the rope didn't move.

"Robard?" I hollered up again.

"Yes?" came the reply.

"We're ready," I repeated.

"I know," he said.

"What are you waiting for?" Maryam shouted.

"I'm just thinking," he said.

"About what?" she yelled back.

"About how much I don't like heights," he said.

Maryam and I looked at each other. Oh no.

"Why didn't you say something?" I cried.

"Because I didn't think you'd actually be crazy enough to try this!" he yelled.

"We can't go back now! Come on!" Maryam shouted up to him.

"It's okay. I think I'll just go around," he said.

Robard stood fifty feet above us, his eyes locked on ours. He didn't move.

"I can't climb down," he said finally.

"Yes, you can!" Maryam assured him.

"No, I can't," he asserted.

Maryam looked at me. "Now what?"

I shrugged. "I have no idea."

"Robard, I know you're scared. But you have to do this," she coaxed. "You'll be fine. Just keep your feet against the cliff and follow the sound of my voice. I'll talk you down."

Robard silently shook his head in defiance.

We were wasting more time, but I couldn't leave him stranded on the side of the mountain. Then I had an idea. Robard had yet to release Maryam's rope and had his own length still looped over his shoulder.

"Robard, remember what I said earlier? Take your rope and loop it around the small boulder." If I could just get him moving, maybe he'd start climbing.

"All right," he said.

"Now tie your rope to the end of Maryam's, put one end around your shoulders and waist, then drop the other end down to us. We'll lower you down. You won't even have to climb!" I tried to put my most reassuring look on my face.

"I don't like the look on your face right now. You look as if you're trying to sell me a lame horse!" he shouted.

"Robard, please . . . I know you're frightened, but we need to get going. Celia won't be able to hold off Sir Hugh forever."

Robard stood still a bit longer, but, gathering his will, slipped the coil of rope over his shoulders. He tied the two ends of the rope together and vanished from sight briefly, then returned to view and tossed the rope to us.

"I'm ready," he said. "But squire, if you drop me, so help me, as soon as I recover from the fall, I will give you a thrashing like you've never imagined."

"What if Maryam drops you?" I asked.

"Don't try to change the subject," he insisted. He backed up toward the very edge of the rocks. Maryam and I took up the slack on the rope, and he slowly inched his way over.

Robard was considerably larger than the two of us, and it took all of our strength to control his descent. But slowly, he climbed farther down the mountainside. Maryam constantly reassured him.

"You're doing fine," she said. "Keep coming, you're almost there."

About twenty feet above us he paused for a moment, frozen in place.

"What's wrong?" I asked.

"Nothing," he said.

"Just a few more feet." Maryam's voice was soothing.

Robard kept backing slowly toward us and I could see he was straining hard. The muscles across his back were hunched, and his legs trembled as he dug into the cliff with his feet.

"Relax," I said. "You've almost got it."

Then the rope went slack in our hands. Robard screamed, and we could only watch in quiet desperation as he lunged away from the wall and fell.

# 25

ook out!" Maryam shouted as she leaned toward the end of the small ledge. With only an instant to think and with Robard almost on top of me, I reached up and grabbed his left arm. He slammed into me, and I tried to take the blow with my back and shoulders so as not to crush Angel.

The force of Robard's impact knocked me to my knees. I struggled mightily to hold on to him in fear of what happened next. His momentum pulled us, and though I strained to keep him on the ledge, the space was too small and he was too heavy.

"Hang on!" I shouted.

I didn't need to tell Robard twice. As he fell past me, he threw his arms around my waist, and we continued to tumble down the side of the mountain until we jerked to a stop and crashed into the wall, knocking the wind out of me. My back ached as though a giant had used it to scrape the mud from his boots.

"Are you all right?" I asked Robard.

"When we get down from here, I am going to kill you," he replied calmly. So he was not seriously injured.

"Are you hurt?" Maryam shouted from the ledge above us.

"No," I answered back.

"Yes!" shouted Robard. Our plunge had woken Angel, and she squirmed against my chest.

"He's not hurt," I said. "He's just mad."

"I just fell off a mountain!" he squealed. "Mad doesn't even begin to describe it! I told you this was a bad idea!"

"Tristan!" Maryam shouted.

"Yes?"

"I think we better do something quickly. There's no telling how long this bush will hold your weight!" She sounded nervous.

"Robard, I'm going to let you go," I said gently.

"What? Oh no you aren't!" he demanded.

"I have to. I can't hold you much longer, and Maryam thinks the bush is going to give way. Don't worry, I'm still tied off, and if we hurry, we can get you the rest of the way down."

"No!" he said.

"Do you have a better idea?" I asked.

"We wait here until help comes," he said.

"Robard, there is no help coming. Maryam is going to need us to get her down. If we hang on like this much longer, the bush *will* break and we'll both be dead. I want you to loop your rope around my waist and I'll lower you down the rest of the way."

Robard didn't move at first, but then one of his hands released the iron grip he held on me and he threaded the rope around my waist.

"Are you ready?" I asked when he had tied his rope to me securely.

"Yes. No. Not really, but I am still going to kill you when we get off this rock," he snarled.

Muttering under his breath, he pushed off with his legs. There was a tremendous feeling of relief at the temporary release of his weight, but when the rope caught again, I wasn't prepared for the strain. I let out an anguished yell as the rope dug into my body.

"What's wrong?" Maryam and Robard both shouted at once.

"Nothing. Keep going!" I said through clenched teeth.

Robard's feet scrabbled at the side of the cliff, but he reached a foothold and rested his weight on it, giving me some relief.

"Ready?" he asked the moment his feet hit the shelf. I was most definitely not. When had Robard become such an eager mountain climber?

"Yes. Go," I said, taking a deep breath.

This time he dropped a few more feet. He was now ten feet below me, and I continually let out more rope. Fifteen feet. Now twenty. He found another resting place, and I nearly cried with joy as he took the weight off the line.

He finally reached the bottom of the cliff. When he stood on firm ground, he let out a whoop, and I pulled the rope from around my waist and hung my head.

A noise from above startled me. Looking up, I almost fell myself, for there was Maryam, her rope tied around her waist, climbing down the cliff. Her feet and hands instantly found every obvious foot- or handhold, and she methodically made her way down.

"What are you doing?" I asked. "What are you tied to?"

"Climbing down. The bush will hold my weight fine," she answered. "I could tell you were in no shape to help me."

Maryam pushed out from the cliff wall, and having twisted a length of the rope around one leg, she let herself down until she was almost even with me.

"Now what?" I asked. She was nearly at the end of her length of rope.

"You concentrate on getting down yourself. I can make it from here on my own."

"But you'll run out of rope," I said.

"No, I won't. We're almost down now. This is easy," she replied.

"How did you learn to do this?" I asked.

Maryam looked at me and smiled. "Hashshashin have many mountain strongholds. There was no doubt I would make it. It was you two I was worried about," she said as if it answered my question.

"Hey, you two! Hurry up," Robard shouted up from below.

I pushed and clawed with my feet at the cliff face. I went slowly—too exhausted and worried my next mistake would be my last. But we had beaten the mountain. Before long, I reached the bottom with Robard and Maryam and collapsed to the ground, leaning my sore back against a convenient boulder. Every part of me ached. I untied the knots in Martine's cape and Angel broke free from her cloth prison. I pulled my tunic over my head. Maryam checked the scrapes and bruises on my back.

"You'll heal," she said. When it came to injuries, Maryam was not overly sympathetic.

Robard's near brush with death had taken a little of the edge off his anger. After five minutes he stopped threatening to kill me "as soon as I was able to stand and face him like a man," and then we all laughed.

"Why are we laughing?" Robard asked.

"I don't know," I said. "It just feels good."

The laughter petered out, and we sat there letting the late morning sun warm us in the face of the cool wind blowing everywhere on the mountain. After a few minutes of rest and some water from our skins, I staggered to my feet. If I sat much longer, I would never get up again, and I wanted to put as much distance between us and Sir Hugh as possible. He would have to go a long way around to reach us, but he was mounted and we were not. There was no time to waste.

The ground was steep here, but we could pick our way through the boulders and rocks lining the way. We were careful, because a fall would still mean a quick tumble down the sharp incline, but we no longer needed the ropes. Two hours later, we reached the valley floor and were once again surrounded by trees and the sounds of the forest.

I looked up at the sun and headed deeper into the woods. Maryam, Robard and Angel fell into step alongside me.

"Which way?" Maryam asked.

"North," I replied. "We're going home."

# 26

very day we hiked from first light until well after sundown. For the first three days, the travel was strenuous as we moved in and out of the mountain valleys. We skirted major farms and villages, and after Celia's supply of food ran out, we foraged for whatever we could find. Sir Hugh would expect us to turn south and head to the coast, so taking the more difficult route would at least cover our tracks for a time.

Robard and Maryam never complained. After a few days, Robard took to circling back to scout for us. Each morning he would take his leave while Maryam and I headed ever northward, and then at nightfall, as if by magic, he found us. Robard was at home in the forest, and although he talked incessantly of returning to Sherwood, he was more content than at any time since I'd met him.

One night Robard returned to our camp with a goose slung over his shoulder and carrying a bundle of birch saplings. He expertly butchered the goose while Maryam made a fire, and before long we had dinner cooking over the flames. Angel sat on her haunches very near the fire, whining and pawing at the dirt and staring hungrily at the meat.

While we rested, Robard inspected the birch saplings, holding them up to his eye as if to judge their straightness. Some he discarded, but in the end he had about a dozen he found suitable.

"What are you doing?" Maryam asked.

"Making arrows," he replied. "We can't go into a town or city, and besides, I wouldn't trust a Frank fletcher anyway. So I've got to make my own. Luckily I found a goose. I've extra points, but no feathers."

Robard pulled a small pouch from his wallet. Inside were arrowheads and a small roll of string. It was interesting to watch him work because he was so meticulous. With his small knife, he carved a notch at the head of the piece of birch until the arrowhead would fit in it precisely. Then he wound the string around the arrowhead, tying it off tightly.

Tying on the feathers was the most difficult and time-consuming part of the job. Robard carefully trimmed a goose feather in half, and when he had three pieces of relatively equal size, he used a bit of tree sap to hold them to the shaft temporarily. He then wound each feather carefully with string, moving it back and forth between the barbs until it was securely fastened.

"There!" he said, holding up the finished masterpiece proudly. "An arrow suitable for a King's Archer." At the mention of the King, of course, Robard spat on the ground.

Each arrow took a few hours to complete. He worked on them for the next several nights while we kept moving north. I had no idea where we were going specifically, only a general sense of direction. All I knew was that England and the Channel lay north of us, so I intended to walk until I reached the sea. I would worry about crossing when I got there. One night, as if reading my mind, Maryam asked how we would reach England.

"Once we arrive at this channel of yours, how do you intend to get us across it?" she asked.

"By ship," I said, with confidence.

"I know by *ship*. But what kind of ship? Where do we find one?"

Robard chuckled under his breath as he worked at completing another arrow.

"Still to be determined," I said.

"In other words, you have no idea, as usual," Maryam said.

"No, I have an *idea*. It will definitely be a boat or ship of some kind," I said resolutely.

Maryam rolled her eyes. "I hate ships," she said, remembering her experience in the storm.

"Me too," I told her. "But we can't walk to England."

In a few days, Robard had managed to replenish his supply of arrows. His wallet was nearly full, but he kept a constant lookout for suitable shafts. Without him I don't know if we would have survived. Each evening he returned from scouting with some type of game so we didn't go hungry. The nights were cool, and sleeping on the ground made us stiff and sore. But after a few days, when it looked as if Sir Hugh might have lost our trail, I felt happier than I had in a long time.

I still thought constantly of Celia. But I enjoyed walking along with Maryam each day, with Angel trotting happily along beside us until she smelled something in the woods and darted after it, barking lustily. Each night, when Robard arrived and told us he had seen no sign of Sir Hugh or anyone else who might be following us, it buoyed my spirits even more.

I hadn't grown careless or forgotten that Sir Hugh would still be coming. But because I had finally unburdened myself to Maryam and Robard, my steps were lighter. The Grail was no longer a millstone around my neck, because I had friends who stood beside me and helped me lift up what had so weighed down my spirits.

Still, we were cautious. Robard watched our backs, and Angel became adept at alerting us if strangers were nearby. She would stop with her head pointed in front of her and sniff the air, then let out a low growl of warning. Maryam and I learned to recognize this pose and what it meant, and when she took it, we would scamper off the trail or find a thicket or stand of trees to hide in. Angel would follow us and stand ready but silent until the danger had passed.

We saw no soldiers or Templars, but many peasants and farmers. Invisibility was the key to our safety, for if no one saw us, then no one could tell Sir Hugh which way we traveled.

After we had been gone from Montségur for nearly three weeks, Robard returned to camp one night with a worried look on his face.

"What is it?" I asked as he strode into the light of our small fire.

"I'm not certain," he said, kneeling to warm his hands by the flames. "I've not seen a soul, but I circled back toward the village we passed last night," he said. "North of there I found signs of a large group of horses headed this way. But I lost their tracks at the river. They must have ridden a ways in the shallows. I couldn't find where they came out on either side. It bothers me how they headed this way first, but then vanished."

"Do you think it might be Sir Hugh?" I wondered.

"I'm not sure. But it was a large group, so it had to be either soldiers or knights. It may be the local baron's fyrd, but I don't like how their tracks disappeared. It means they're trying to conceal themselves. Why would the local fyrd act so?"

Neither Maryam nor I had an answer. At nightfall we agreed to take turns standing watch. Robard was still full of energy from his scout, so he volunteered to go first. Maryam would stand second, then wake me for the final hours until morning. Despite the tension and worry, I lay down near the fire, Angel settling in next to me, and fell asleep instantly.

Maryam shook me awake after her watch. I was groggy and out of sorts, having never been a person who wakes easily from sleep. Angel rolled over as Maryam took my spot on the ground, then settled next to her and was quickly back to sleep.

I squatted by the fire to warm myself, then stood, trying to ease the soreness out of my legs. The woods were quiet, and I guessed we had about three hours till sunrise. Robard lay on the other side of the fire, opposite Maryam, snoring quietly. His bow and wallet leaned against a tree next to him. I had slept with the short sword and battle sword close by, and I shrugged my way into them, still trying to come fully awake.

For a few minutes I paced around the edge of camp, stopping to listen to the sounds of the night. I heard nothing out of the ordinary. After half an hour I grew bored. Robard's news had me on edge. I leaned with my back against the trunk of a tall tree and looked up at the sky. It was an overcast evening, and only the small flicker of flame provided any light.

Perhaps I could gather some more wood and build the fire up a bit. But before I could move, an arm came from behind the tree and a hand clamped over my mouth. I tried to shout out a warning, but only a slight grunt escaped.

Then it seemed as if the darkness exploded into movement. Maryam screamed and several man-sized shapes converged on the fire. Maryam rolled to her feet and ran out of the small circle of light, disappearing into the blackness. Robard shouted curses, and Angel became a symphony of barks and snarls.

My hand tried desperately to pull my short sword, but another arm clamped mine in place. I was helpless in the strong grip of my assailant. I twisted my head back and forth, and when I felt one of the fingers tear at my cheek, I bit down hard. A yelp sounded from behind me and I was momentarily released.

I pushed off the tree and darted toward the fire. Robard was being dragged away, and I raised my sword and shouted "Beauseant!" at the top of my lungs. Something hit me hard in the back and I went down. Try as I might, I couldn't throw the weight off me. I tried to push myself up on my hands and knees, but was clubbed in the back of the head and down I went, losing my sword. The campfire was only a few inches away. I bucked up with all my might and felt my attacker fall to the side.

Grabbing a burning log from the campfire, I stood and swung where I thought the man should be, but he wasn't. Confused,

I turned around and had only a second with the light from the flaming log to see him standing in front of me. He held the hilt of his sword tight in his hand, and before it connected with the side of my head and everything faded to blackness, I recognized his uniform.

These were not Templars.

They were King's Guards.

# 27

s I swam up toward consciousness, I sensed we were being carried up and down over rough ground. There were voices quietly murmuring around me. It sounded like Maryam and Robard, but I couldn't be sure. Finally, I managed to open my eyes and looked up to see the sun peeking down at me through the bars of a cage.

A ripple of dizziness overtook me as I tried to sit up. "Easy, Tristan," I heard Maryam say. Her hands probed the side of my head. The attack in the woods came flashing back to me, along with the last thing I remembered—turning to see the King's Guard seconds before he punched me in the head.

"Where are we?" I mumbled.

"We don't know," Maryam said. "We're locked inside a cage on the back of a wagon. We've been traveling for several hours now."

My head was resting in Maryam's lap. I finally opened my eyes and willed myself to stay focused. The dizziness passed, and I gingerly pulled myself into a sitting position. I touched the side of my face and winced.

"Careful," Maryam said. "You've got a nasty knot there."

When I could finally focus, I squinted up at the sun. We were still heading north.

"What happened?" I asked, still confused. I remembered someone grabbing me from behind as I stood next to the tree, and then everything else became a blur. Looking through the bars of our cage, I counted ten of Richard the Lionheart's personal soldiers riding alongside us. Two sat on the wagon, driving the team, and the rest were on horseback, surrounding us as we moved along the bumpy road.

Something wasn't right. I wouldn't have been surprised if it had been a regimento of Templars or even the High Counsel's men. Even though Sir Hugh had belittled and intimidated him, maybe he was able to separate himself from Sir Hugh and follow us. But King's Guards? Could Sir Hugh have enlisted their aid? The last I'd known, King Richard was in Outremer, so why was there a detachment of King's Guards here in France? Was Prince John or some other member of the royal family here? Did Sir Hugh's connections reach all the way to the throne? Did this have something to do with my previous run-ins with them?

It was hard to believe. It had been more than a year ago when they'd stalked me through the marketplace in Dover. But as I studied their faces, I didn't recognize any of these men. There was something else at work here.

"Maryam, Robard," I stammered. "I'm sorry. I guess this is my fault. They were on me before I saw or heard them. They must have come upwind from Angel or else she would have smelled them and warned . . . Where is Angel?" I noticed her absence for the first time.

"She ran off," Maryam said.

"Ran off?" I couldn't believe it. Angel, who had jumped into the harbor, survived a shipwreck, attacked a Frenchman, and was carried haphazardly down a mountainside, had simply disappeared?

Maryam nodded. "I know. One of those men knocked her aside during the scuffle and she scurried off into the woods."

I shook my head and immediately wished I hadn't, for the world began swirling again.

"Maryam?" I whispered.

"Yes?"

"What is wrong with Robard? Why hasn't he said anything?" I asked, looking over at Robard, who squatted on the floor of the cage opposite us with his back to me. His body was coiled and he held on to the bars as if he might shake them apart if given the chance.

"I think he's angry," she said.

"Yes, he's angry. But usually when he's in a temper, he reminds me how he'll kill me after we get through this."

"Perhaps he is *very* angry," she suggested.

"If you must know," Robard interrupted, "I am studying our enemies."

"To what end?" I asked him.

"I don't know yet," he said.

They had stripped us of our weapons and my satchel and piled them in the wagon behind the driver and his mate, far out of reach from the cage. A weapon would be useless in the small, enclosed space, and I couldn't fathom what advantage Robard thought he might gain, locked away as we were.

With nothing else to do, I sat quietly as the wagon rolled along. It was rough riding, and as the sun moved toward the west, it became even more uncomfortable, bouncing along in the heat. A short while later, the Captain of the Guard gave halt, and the men dismounted, leading the horses to a small spring. One of the men on the wagon seat got down from his perch and pushed a water skin through the bars, offering it first to Maryam.

She lowered her head while reaching for it, then quickly rose up and reached through the bars, grabbing the man by the wrist and twisting it sharply to the side. He screamed in pain, dropping the water skin. As the man struggled to free himself from Maryam's grip, she reached out with her other hand and twisted his thumb backward. We heard a sickening pop and the man screeched again, finally yanking his hand away from Maryam's grasp.

"Swine!" she yelled, spitting at him.

The man howled, struggling to pull his sword with his good hand. The other guards watched and jeered now as the man thrust it through the bars at Maryam, who easily ducked out of the way.

He cursed at her, protesting his broken thumb. But he couldn't move his sword quickly between the bars, and before I knew it, Robard had leapt forward and wrestled it from the man's hand.

"Robard, no!" I shouted.

Moving like a cat, he reached through the bars, grabbing the man by his tunic first, pushing him backward, then slamming him headfirst into the side of the cage. The man groaned and slumped toward the ground, but Robard held him up, turning him and putting his left arm through the bars and around the man's neck. He held the sword at the now unconscious man's throat.

"Release us now, or he dies!" Robard commanded.

All of the guards drew their weapons, then stood still, not sure what to do.

The Captain of the Guard strode over to the wagon and stood a few feet away, his sword pointed down at the ground.

"Let him go," the Captain said quietly. He removed his helmet and held it in his free hand. His beard was dark brown, and he was covered head to toe in dust and mud from the ride. His hands were gnarled and scarred, and it looked like his fingers had been cut or broken many times. He was definitely someone we shouldn't trifle with.

"Not until you unlock the cage and return our weapons," Robard said.

The Captain sighed. "You won't kill him," he said.

"What? I surely will!" Robard replied, more than a little put out.

"Were you a Crusader?" the Captain asked.

"I was. What of it? Quit trying to stall us! Open the cage and let us go or your man dies," Robard insisted.

"You were a King's Archer? Your bow is a fine weapon. Is it Welsh-made, by any chance? I've always heard how Welshmen make the best archers," the Captain said nonchalantly.

"Welsh? Welsh, my arse! A Welshman couldn't hit the ocean from a boat. That's English yew there. The finest there is. Now, I've had enough of your games. Open this cage and release us." Robard tightened his grip and pushed the sword deeper into the man's neck.

The Captain sighed again. His eyes were tired and world weary, but they glinted with determination. Instantly, I knew he would let his man die before he freed the three of us. He stared at Robard.

"I'm afraid I can't do that," he said quietly.

"Do it now!" Robard commanded.

"No," the Captain answered.

"I'll kill him!" Robard shouted.

"Then do it. But you're not going free," the Captain said.

Robard's face fell and his eyes narrowed. Maryam and I sat slumped in the cage, too stunned to say anything. Time went by without a sound from anyone except the ragged breathing of the unconscious guard. Finally, Robard saw the same thing in the Captain's eyes I had. He reluctantly tossed the sword to the ground.

The Captain gestured to two of his men, who stepped forward and took the guard from Robard's grasp. They lifted him up onto the wagon seat where he sat slumped against the driver, who took up the reins.

"Mount up!" the Captain commanded, and shortly we were back on our way. The Captain and the guards rode on, undisturbed by what had just happened.

Robard pounded his fists against the iron bars in frustration. "I smell your friend Sir Hugh," he said.

"I'm not sure, Robard," I mused. "I'm certain he would have headed for the southern coast first. We were careful as we traveled north. . . ." I let my words trail off. In truth, I did not know what to think.

For the rest of the afternoon, we rode on without stopping. We had kept the water skin inside the cage and passed it around a few times. There was little conversation as we rolled along. Since we had left Montségur those many days ago and walked ever northward, I had assumed we would reach the northern coast eventually, but I had no idea how much country there was to cross or how long it would take us. Now as our small band kept moving along, a familiar smell came to me. I sat up, taking a sniff of the air.

"What is it?" Maryam asked.

"I think . . . it's the . . ." I still wasn't sure.

Then the forest cleared, and a small city shadowed by a large castle lying along the seacoast came into view.

"We're at the ocean," I said. "I don't know which town this is or what part of the coast we're on, but we must be at the Channel."

Robard and Maryam were not cheered by the news, and given the circumstances, I couldn't blame them.

Within a half hour we pulled inside the castle. As the gate was wheeled shut, the guards dismounted and several grooms hurried forward to take their horses to the stables. The driver of the wagon unlocked the cage door with an iron key.

"Welcome to Calais," said the Captain of the Guard. "Step lively now."

My head still throbbed as we climbed out of the cage, but it was almost delightful to no longer be jounced around. Two guards took me by the arms, others followed suit for Maryam and Robard, and with the Captain at the head of our small column, we were led into the castle keep. They led us down a long, dimly lit hall and into a large room, brightly decorated with red carpets and brilliantly colored tapestries hanging on the walls. At the end of the room was a large wooden chair raised on a platform. Behind the chair was a beautiful purple velvet screen.

The chair was occupied by a commanding-looking woman. Her long, dark brown hair was splashed with gray, and the lines on her face said she'd spent much time in the sun and wind. But her eyes were dark and lively, and they glowed when she saw us. She looked us over as we approached, her gaze finally settling on me.

We were led all the way across the room until we were only a few feet from the chair.

"Kneel before the Queen Mother," the Captain commanded.

The Queen Mother? Eleanor of Aquitaine? I had heard stories of her. She was King Henry's queen and Richard the Lionheart's mother. What was she doing here, and more important, why were the three of us being brought before her?

We stood as still as statues, unsure what to do.

"I said kneel!" the Captain commanded. The calm demeanor he had exhibited in the woods was gone. Being around the Queen Mother made him more forceful, and there was a tinge of cruelty in his tone. Our guards kicked at the backs of our knees, forcing us to the ground.

Queen Eleanor stood silently from her chair, studying us intently. Then she spoke.

"Sir Hugh? Are these the three?" Sir Hugh stepped around the velvet screen and stood next to but slightly behind her. He smiled his serpent's smile when he saw me. I was surprised, but not shocked, to find him here. No matter where I went, he kept turning up.

"The very same, my lady," he said.

Eleanor of Aquitaine nodded slightly, and the corners of her mouth moved upward just a tick. She stepped down from the platform to look carefully at Robard, then Maryam, until finally she stood directly in front of me. She was a small woman and used the platform to make herself more imposing. Bending over until her face was inches from my own, she appeared to memorize my every feature.

"Delicious," she said with a wicked smile. "Delicious."

# CALAIS, FRANCE
## DECEMBER 1191

# 28

ueen Eleanor turned her back to me and stepped up onto the platform, settling on her throne. Sir Hugh had a look of vast relief on his face. He had lost us at Montségur and by his own clumsy efforts had been unable to find us again. I wondered, though, why he had aligned himself with the Queen Mother.

"From what Sir Hugh tells me, you're a slippery one, young squire," she said as she stared at me. Instinct told me she wasn't on my side, but I had no idea what she was talking about.

"Forgive me, your highness, but I'm not sure what you mean," I told her.

To my surprise, Eleanor threw back her head and laughed. Or cackled rather. It was unsettling to say the least.

"Please, boy. Do you pretend ignorance of your circumstances?" she said.

"I have many circumstances, my lady. Which one are you referring to?"

Sir Hugh started toward me with his fist raised. "You'll not take such a tone with the Queen Mother, boy!" But Eleanor held out her hand, touching him gently on the arm before he reached me.

"Not now, Hugh," she said. Sir Hugh stepped back to his place behind her and sulked.

"I'm referring to the circumstances of your birth," she said.

"If you mean I am an orphan, yes, I'm well aware of it," I said.

"An orphan?" She looked at me quizzically, then threw her head back and laughed again. "An orphan. Oh, how rich this is. Even better than I thought!"

I was at a loss. She appeared more than a little crazy. Sitting up in her chair, her feet twitched nervously beneath the long beaded gown she wore.

"What do you want with us?" Robard demanded, having grown weary of Eleanor's theatrics.

She paused in her study of me to turn her attention to Robard.

"Such impertinence," she said. "Do you know who I am?"

Robard gave her an unfriendly smile and bowed slightly. "Of course I do. You're the mother of a coward who calls himself the Lionheart. Lionheart, my arse! Ha! They ought to call him the Weaselheart instead!" Robard twisted his head as if to spit but thought better of it, given the lush red carpeting we knelt on.

Eleanor's eyes darkened. "Captain," she said, pointing to Robard and Maryam, "put these two in chains. The squire stays here."

The guards pulled Robard and Maryam to their feet. Robard managed to kick one of the guards in the knee and he went down, but another guard drove his fist into Robard's stomach, and he slumped forward with a groan.

"Leave them alone! It's me you want!" I shouted, trying to stand, but the two guards behind me held me down. Robard and Maryam were summarily dragged out of the room. Sir Hugh stood there smiling while the Queen Mother wiggled on her chair. Behind me I heard the fidgeting creak of chain mail from the Captain and the two guards.

"It is you we have wanted for quite some time," Eleanor said.

Me they wanted? She kept behaving as if she knew me, but how could it be so? Then I thought of home, and St. Alban's. And the note I carried in my satchel that the brothers had found tucked into my blue blanket. The abbot had always believed I was born a noble. Could it be? I remembered the words of that note, "Brothers, he is innocent. . . ."

Ridiculous, I told myself. This was only, could only be about the Grail. I was more certain than ever that Sir Hugh was behind this chicanery.

She settled back in her chair and looked at me, her chin in her hand. Her fingers were adorned with large rings that were far too big for her tiny hands. I tried my best to hold her gaze, but I was too tired and sore to care anymore. It was over, they had won. I was done.

"Nothing to say?" she asked.

"Your highness, I would suggest you let me take him to the dungeon and question him," Sir Hugh said.

"There's no rush, Sir Hugh. I'd like to enjoy this for a while. After all, we've been searching for him for fifteen years."

My head came up. Fifteen years searching for me? And she had yet to say anything about the Grail. Could it be she didn't know? Maybe Sir Hugh had kept his true purpose hidden from her as well? She made it sound like it was me she was after. Could I use this knowledge to our advantage somehow?

"Yes, your highness, I have something to say. Has Sir Hugh

told you why he was so desperate to track me down? I assume he asked for your help and the help of your guards?" I asked. The Queen Mother did not answer, but her expression and quick sideways glance at Sir Hugh told me I had hit the mark. "It's because Sir Hugh is quite incompetent. Did he tell you he has pursued me all the way from Outremer yet has never quite managed to catch me? Or did he even tell you why he's chasing me in the first place?"

Eleanor stood up and paced along the wooden platform. Sir Hugh clenched his fists and gritted his teeth.

"Shut your mouth, squire," he spat.

Eleanor watched the exchange with a new curiosity, but said nothing.

"Interesting," I said. "You should ask him . . ."

Sir Hugh shot forward and backhanded me across the face. The blow staggered me, and I fell backward, my legs tucked awkwardly beneath me. I struggled to rise, but Sir Hugh stood over me and raised his fist to strike me again. "I'll teach you proper respect if it's the last thing . . . ," he growled.

"Hugh! Cease!" Eleanor's sharp command stayed his fist in midair. He stood up, straightening his tunic. I struggled to right myself and finally found my balance again, resting my hands on my thighs as I knelt there, feeling the anger rise, tasting blood on my lip. I had been raised by gentle men with no violence in their hearts, but rage grew inside me. At that instant I wanted only to strike Sir Hugh down.

He returned to his spot by Eleanor's throne, but his face betrayed his emotions. Once again he had what he most desired within his grasp, but the powerful Queen Mother stood in his way. If she discovered his true intent, she would undoubtedly relieve him of the Grail.

"How does it feel to always be finishing second, Sir Hugh?" I taunted him. "You couldn't command your own regimento. Sir Thomas was the one the men followed. You wouldn't stand up to the Marshal in Tyre and couldn't defeat a group of peasants at Montségur. Now the Queen Mother pulls your strings. It must be a sad life being such a puppet."

Sir Hugh moved toward me again, but this time Eleanor stood between us.

"He has the same tart tongue as well as the looks," she said. "No wonder Richard sent word to me right away." Again her words only confused me. I had met Richard only twice in passing, not counting saving him on the battlefield. Had Sir Hugh told her of my encounters with her son? Seeing the look of bewilderment on my face, it was as if she read my mind.

"Oh yes, young squire. I know *quite* a lot about you," she said. She clasped her hands in front of her and steepled her fingers. "Quite a lot indeed. And I'm sure you must have many questions."

I hesitated. The Grail was my only advantage here. If I told her of its existence, I could thwart Sir Hugh, but giving it to her might be worse. I waited.

"Questions, squire? I can see them on your face. Don't you wish to know? About your past?"

It felt as if she had punched me in the stomach. Trying not to show any interest, I straightened and threw my shoulders back. Of course I wished to know. But I would never give her the satisfaction. Not while she held my friends in her dungeon. Not ever. Besides, this had to be about the Grail. If Sir Hugh had told her I was an orphan, of my encounters with her son, then I was certain she was taking some perverse delight in tormenting me. Maybe, just maybe, she was the one who wanted the Grail and had sent Sir Hugh to find it, promising him something he desired when he delivered it to her. Sir Thomas' warnings about the greed and madness of those who had dedicated their lives to finding it floated through my mind. I told myself there was nothing she could do to me that would cause me to break my vow to my knight or my friends.

She only laughed at me, in her ridiculous high-pitched cackle. Witch.

"Captain, take him to the dungeon with his friends," she commanded. "Sir Hugh and I have much to discuss."

The guards pulled me to my feet.

"If it pleases my lady, I will accompany the guards to ensure he is safely locked away," Sir Hugh said.

The Queen Mother waved him away with her hand. "Fine. Do so, but return here at once. And I mean immediately, Hugh."

We left the room, walking down a long passageway that ended at a heavy wooden door. It creaked open, and a stone stairway led us down to a single cell that had been dug out of the ground. The door opened and I was unceremoniously pushed in. There was only one flickering torch lighting the cavern, and I could barely make out Robard and Maryam sitting slumped against the wall, their hands and feet shackled in chains. The iron door slammed behind me and I heard the key turn. Before I could step back, Sir Hugh reached through the bars, grabbing hold of my tunic, and slammed me forward so my face was only inches away from his.

He lowered his voice and hissed, "Where is it, squire?"

"Why should I tell you now? You're going to kill me anyway." I spoke loudly, hoping the Captain and his guards would hear me and wonder what Sir Hugh was talking about.

Sir Hugh smirked and released me.

"Captain, where are their belongings?" he asked.

"Still in the wagon, sire," the Captain replied.

"Bring them to me at once," he barked. He released his grip on me and left, nearly racing up the few steps. The Captain and his guards followed, and we heard the wooden door slam and lock.

They hadn't even put me in chains. Robard and Maryam both stood. Their hands were bound and locked in front of them, and a long chain ran between the shackles on their hands to their feet, but they could stand and move about a bit. Luckily the walls of the dungeon were just dirt and they were not chained to the wall.

"How are we going to get out of here?" Robard asked.

"I don't know," I answered.

I gave the cell door a shake, but it was locked securely.

Up above us a single barred window let in fresh air.

"Does anyone have any ideas?" I begged. Robard and Maryam were silent.

Then I heard a scratching sound at the window above. We looked up and the three of us were startled to see Angel's face poking through the bars of the window. In her mouth she clutched Robard's belt, on which he carried a small knife. She let go of the belt and it tumbled to the floor at our feet.

Then she yipped happily.

espite our desperate situation, the three of us were so overjoyed to see the dog that we all laughed out loud. Robard in particular was beside himself, whistling and praising her repeatedly. For a moment I wondered if he might have taken too many blows to the head in his struggles with the King's Guards.

With the knife, I tried unlocking Robard and Maryam's wrist shackles and leg irons. The locks' chains were too thick and rusty for me to have any success. It would require a hammer and chisel to release them.

Having no luck with the chains, I tried inserting the knife into the lock on the cell door to see if I could work it open. Slowly, I twisted and turned the knife for several minutes but to no avail. I pounded on the bar nearest me in frustration. How could I get us out of here?

The dog answered with a quiet bark and dug at the base of one of the bars in the window. Not understanding her meaning, I stood there stupidly at first. She barked again and continued digging, whining and growling as she did so.

Then it came to me.

"Robard, Maryam, you're going to have to boost me up," I said, crossing to the window. They shuffled over and made a platform for my feet with their hands. I stepped onto it, and they hoisted me up until I was level with the opening.

There was almost no light to work with, as the flame from the torch outside the cell barely reached here. But Angel whined again, digging around the bar, and feeling there with my fingers, I found that the mortar had worked loose. While I attacked it with the knife, she sat back to watch me work.

"Keep an eye out, girl," I said. "Let me know if anyone comes this way."

I worked the knife into the soft mortar around the iron bar. It was tough going, but little by little, small chunks fell away. After a few minutes the bar began to twist in my hand, cracking and loosening more mortar. When a big piece came loose at the bottom, I lay down the knife and grabbed it with both hands, pulling and twisting at the bar until the bottom snapped out and I yanked it free. Ha!

Robard and Maryam had adjusted their positions, so I stood on their thighs while they balanced me as best they could with chained hands.

"Quit goofing around, squire," Robard groused. "You're heavy!"

If I could loosen one more bar, we might have enough space to wiggle our way to freedom. With large sections of mortar missing from the first bar, I could get better leverage with my knife. I worked the bottom free and pulled until it broke loose in my hand. I wanted to shout but was leery of alerting anyone. Grasping the remaining two bars, I pulled myself up and wiggled through the window. Angel was so happy she nearly attacked me.

"Easy, girl," I said. On my hands and knees, I poked my head back through the bars, reaching down for Maryam. She took my hand and had just enough give in her shackles to place her foot up on the wall, grasp the bar and lift herself up. She squirmed her way through and lay there on the ground while Angel welcomed her in her own particular fashion.

"Robard, you're next," I said as I reached down for him. He took my arm in both hands and dug his boots into the stone wall. It was damp and smooth, and with his feet chained, hard for him to get a toehold.

"Push!" I groaned as he inched his way up the wall.

"Don't yell at me to push, Templar! You're the one who got us into this! It's not easy trying to climb when your feet are chained together!" Robard was still in a temper and I couldn't blame him. I *had* gotten us into this mess. But I was doing my best to get us out. Robard kicked and groaned and strained, but finally wormed his way through.

If Angel had been happy to see Maryam and me, she was overjoyed to see Robard. She jumped on his chest and he sat up, scooping her up in his arms and hugging her to his chest. "I missed you too, girl," he said, chuckling.

We had no time to lose. We were now in the bailey of the castle, hidden in the shadows of the wall. Robard and Maryam could stand and walk in a shuffling step by holding on to the chain connecting their hands and feet.

"What's our next step?" Maryam asked.

"Escaping? I vote for escaping," said Robard.

"Yes, but first things first: we have to get those shackles off. I need to check on something though," I said, spotting the wagon that had carried us here parked nearby.

The bailey, essentially a large courtyard in this castle, was cluttered with other wagons and stacks of barrels and equipment, and in the lengthening shadows, I covertly made my way to the wagon and peeked over the side. Our weapons were gone, as was my satchel. My heart sank. Sir Hugh had likely discovered the Grail by now. He was probably dancing with glee.

My feet felt leaden as I made my way back to the wall.

"Nothing?" Robard said.

"No, everything's gone," I said.

"Sir Hugh must have them. I say we find weapons and take our possessions back," Robard said.

"Robard, we can't attack a castle full of King's Guards. They are sworn to defend the Queen Mother to the death. We need to get out of here first. Sir Hugh will leave at some point and we can follow him," I reasoned.

"Given our history together, I almost hate to ask, but do you have any idea of how to get these chains off of us?" Maryam said.

"Yes. With this many horses they have to have a blacksmith. Let's find the forge. With a hammer and chisel we can get them off easily. Come on," I said.

We kept to the wall and made our way along it until we had circled the courtyard. Everything appeared deserted. Angel sniffed the air. "Is anyone there, girl?" I asked as if she could understand me.

Silently she crept ahead of us, her nose constantly working the air. Then she darted into the stables and vanished from sight. We looked at each other, unsure what to do. Seconds later she was back. With a quiet bark she ran toward the door, stopped, and looked at us again, as if imploring us to follow. We hurried over to the door and slipped through to find it empty.

The interior was lit by oil lamps, and it was far bigger even than the one in Acre. At least a dozen stalls were on each side, almost all of them filled with horses. As I had hoped, at the rear wall sat an anvil next to a forge and bench with blacksmith tools. In a few moments I had freed them both.

"I say we each take a horse and ride out of here," Robard said.

I shook my head. "I'm fairly certain the Queen Mother doesn't know what Sir Hugh is up to concerning the Grail. There is something else at work here. I need to know what it is."

Just then we were interrupted by a series of shouts from the courtyard outside. Maryam ran to the door and peeked out. "I think they've discovered our escape," she said. We could hear the sounds of running feet and orders being shouted to the guards and men-at-arms.

"Too bad we don't have our weapons. With my bow, I'm sure we could make it to the gate at least," Robard said.

Robard's idea of taking the horses sounded more appealing. As I tried to decide our next move, Angel rose up on her back feet and pawed at my hip, whining and growling at me. I pushed her away. "Not now, girl," I told her. She left my side and moved over to the first stall inside the stable door, which was piled high with hay. She pounced on the pile and dug at it furiously, and soon bits of straw were flying all about.

"What is she doing?" Maryam asked.

Angel yanked at something buried under the straw. She growled and finally pulled something free. I recognized it instantly. It was my satchel. Robard ran to the stall and kicked aside a large pile of hay.

There on the floor lay our weapons.

e looked in wonder at what Angel had done. She sat on her haunches, watching us expectantly. She had managed to follow us all the way to Calais and sneak her way into the castle. Robard's bow and wallet, Maryam's daggers and my satchel and short sword were all there. The only thing missing was Sir Thomas' battle sword, which I could only assume was too heavy for her to move.

Taking her in my arms, I nuzzled her cheek while she licked my face. At that moment I truly missed the brothers of St. Alban's, for I would have loved to tell them about my guardian angel who took the shape of a small golden dog. I wished then I had a spit full of meat for her to eat.

"If I hadn't seen it with my own eyes, I never would have believed it," Robard said as he shrugged into his wallet and strung his bow.

Maryam reached down to pick up her daggers and wiped the handles on her tunic. "Indeed," she said, smiling. "Allah shines his grace on our little friend." I put Angel back on the ground and reached inside the satchel, nearly fainting with relief to find the Grail still in place.

"We need to get out of here," Robard said, his voice full of tension. We peered out of the stable door, viewing the activity in the courtyard. Across the way, near the entrance to the keep, two squads of King's Guards were forming up, torches were being lit all around the compound, and soon they'd search the grounds inch by inch. All of them were heavily armed, and I could see Sir Hugh in the shadows in an animated discussion with the Captain, waving his arms about, no doubt promising horrors beyond imagination if we were not found.

Robard led us quietly out of the stable, and keeping to the castle wall, the four of us trotted silently along it, making our way toward the main gate. When we were close enough to see it, we learned to our distress that it was still closed and guarded by four men.

"Of all the rotten luck!" Robard muttered. "There better be another way out. I couldn't shoot them all before one of them sounded the alarm."

We had to move quickly or we would be trapped. Sir Hugh was banking on the fact that we were still inside the castle, and we wouldn't be able to dodge them forever.

In the corner of the castle wall, between the stables and the gate, was a stone stairway leading to the battlements above. "If we can make it up there without being seen, we might be able to scale down the wall," I said.

"Are you crazy?" Robard snorted. "It's a good twenty feet to the ground. If we fall, we'll be lucky not to bust both legs. And what about her?" he said, gesturing to Angel.

It was immediately clear I hadn't thought this all the way through.

"Wait! In the stables, there was a long coil of rope. We can use it to climb down! I'll be right back," Maryam said. She sprinted back along the wall in the direction we had come.

"Maryam! No!" Robard whispered. He went after her, but I put my arm out to stop him.

"Hold," I said. "Let's wait until we see what happens. Maryam is stealthy. She might be able . . ." I let my words trail off. I could feel the tension in Robard's arm and realized then how much he'd come to care for her. I knew how Maryam felt about him. It was evident every time she looked at him. But I'd not realized it about Robard until now.

In silence, we watched as she slid quickly along in the shadows of the wall and in seconds had slipped through the door of the stables. With rising panic, we watched four of the King's Guards crossing the courtyard toward the stables. Robard started after her again, and it took all my strength to pull him back into the shadows.

"Robard, stop!" I whispered. "Wait to see what happens first. It does no good for all of us to be recaptured." They were certain to find her, and knowing Maryam, she would most likely fight to the death.

Our worst fears were confirmed when a loud commotion rose inside the stable. We heard shouts, and then came a ululating scream and the clang of steel. Robard pulled an arrow from his wallet and nocked it. The doors to the stable burst open, and three of the guards came out carrying a twisting and thrashing Maryam. The fourth guard never appeared.

Robard raised his bow and took aim, but I pushed his arm aside. He whirled on me, and for a moment I thought he might shoot me instead. He was coiled and angry, and I held up my hands.

"Robard, wait. Don't shoot. You might hit her. We'll get her back, I promise. But we have to have a plan."

"I hit what I aim for, Templar!" he snarled, but he released the tension in his bow. Maryam was half dragged, half carried to the center of the bailey where the Captain waited with Sir Hugh. When the guards reached them, they put Maryam on her feet. We were too far away to hear what was said, but without warning Sir Hugh backhanded Maryam across the face and she slumped in the arms of the guards.

Robard cursed and raised his bow again, but realized his folly and lowered it. Angel growled and slunk away in the shadows.

"Think of something, Tristan! Quickly! They'll kill her," he said. My thoughts were frozen in my head, and I was scared and didn't know what to do next.

Maryam still stood slumped in the arms of the two guards, her head bobbing on her chest. The Captain shouted orders, and a wagon with a wooden windlass on its back rolled forward. It was probably used for loading and unloading supplies. One guard threw a rope over the crossbeam, and two others rolled a barrel beneath it. A noose was fastened from the end of the rope, and the two guards raised Maryam up on the barrel and placed the noose around her neck.

Sir Hugh cupped his hands to his mouth and shouted, "Squire! Now is the time to surrender!"

They were going to hang Maryam.

aryam came awake with a jolt and looked about frantically, then settled herself. She shouted at Sir Hugh, but the guards rocked the barrel back and forth and she nearly fell off it. If she did, it would instantly break her neck. She struggled to regain her balance. Then the barrel righted and she stood still on top of it. Robard cursed them for tormenting her. "They're all dead," he muttered under his breath.

"Do you hear me, squire?" Sir Hugh shouted. "Come forward now or your friend dies!"

Sweat poured down my face as I leaned back against the cool stone wall.

"You need to give it to him," Robard said.

"Yes, I know, Robard. But if I give it to him now, he'll kill her anyway. We need leverage. Something we can trade."

"What? We have nothing. Do you understand? Maryam is going to die," he pleaded. It was unsettling to hear Robard talk like this. He was begging me for her life.

Then an idea came to me.

"Robard? Can you shoot the rope?"

"What? Shoot the rope? Of course not! I mean, I'm sure I could if I could get closer, but why?"

"You have to be sure. Can you shoot it? If you were to work your way up behind the wagon over there, you'd be less than thirty yards away. Could you make the shot from such a distance?"

"That's it? That's your plan? For me to get closer and shoot the rope? They'll just kill her with a sword anyway."

"Yes. No. I mean, it's only part of the plan. Can you do it?" Robard removed his wallet and ran his hand through the feathers of his arrows. He removed one a bit longer than the others, with a broader arrowhead. He held it up, sighting along it as if inspecting it for defects. He nocked it in his bow and said, "Yes, I can make the shot. You'll have to give me three or four seconds to stand, draw and sight. But I'll do it."

"Good. Then wait for my signal," I said. Most of the guards had clustered in the courtyard, delaying their search of the grounds to see what happened next.

"All right. When I leave, you make your way to the wagon. Make sure none of the guards up on the battlements can see you clearly. They may have archers up there."

"Leave? What do you mean, leave?" he asked.

"I'm going to get us something to trade," I said.

The castle had enclosed towers on each corner, but to my advantage, the guardhouses were built so the guards could see out, not into the interior. I would be out of their sight lines if I was careful. Leaving Robard still sputtering behind the barrels, I sprinted for the corner stairway. Within seconds I was above the courtyard.

"Squire! I'm telling you, your friend will hang at my command unless you surrender this instant!" Sir Hugh bellowed from down

221

below. He was bluffing. He wouldn't hang Maryam until he knew for sure we were still in the castle. If he did let her die before he got his hands on the Grail, he undoubtedly knew Robard would shoot him at the first opportunity. Sir Hugh was nothing if not a coward. Still I had no time to waste.

As I moved across the rampart, I stayed close to the crenature, which provided me with cover. My brown tunic blended well with the castle stone. I wondered about Robard's progress below, but there was no time to check. In a few seconds, I reached the shadows of the far corner. To my right now was a door into the second level of the keep. I hoped it wasn't locked and made fast toward it, pulling up at the door, pushing against it with my hip.

"Squire, I grow weary of this!" I heard Sir Hugh call out from down below. "I give you to the count of one hundred to show yourself or she hangs!" Luckily the door made no sound. If I was right and Sir Hugh had ordered every available guard outside to search, my plan was going to work. I needed his cooperation, and counted on his greed to possess the Grail.

Once inside there was another stone stairway leading to the upper levels. I gambled the Queen Mother's quarters would be on the top floor. She would demand the most commanding view in the castle. I raced up the two levels of stone steps and stopped, peeking out into the corridor of the top floor. My luck was holding, for a single guard was standing outside a door in the middle of the hallway. I pulled my sword out but carried it down along my leg, where it was concealed in the folds of my tunic. Then I burst into the hallway, running full tilt toward him.

"Guard! The Captain demands you go at once to the bailey! The criminals have been located!" He faced me, momentarily confused.

His hand went to the sword at his belt. "Halt—" he started to say, but now I was upon him and swung the hilt of my sword up, driving it into his chin. With my momentum, the blow lifted him off his feet, and his eyes rolled inward as he landed hard on the ground.

I pushed at the door with all my weight and it swung open, revealing the Queen Mother's chambers. The room was brightly lit by oil lamps, and behind a beautiful oak table she sat. She must have heard the commotion in the hallway, but her face was serene. Behind her stood two of her ladies-in-waiting, and their hands flew to their mouths at the sight of the ruffian who had barged into their ladies' chamber.

When the Queen Mother recognized me, her eyes went dark. Though she tried to hide it, the color drained from her face and she bolted to her feet.

"What is the meaning of this?" she demanded.

Rushing up to the table, I pointed my sword directly at her.

"Your highness, your presence is required in the bailey at once," I told her.

"I'm not going anywhere with you, boy!" she spat.

"My lady, they are about to hang my friend and I have no time to stand on formality. Now, it's your choice: come with me willingly or so help me God, I will drag you down there."

"I'll see *you* hang for this!" she shouted.

"I'll hang anyway! Now move!" As I feinted a thrust across the table with my sword, the Queen Mother stumbled backward with a squawk. Only the quick action of one of her attendants kept her from falling to the ground. Grabbing her arm, I pushed her toward the door.

"Let go of me! How dare you lay your filthy hands on me!" she shouted, clawing at my hand.

Before leaving, I warned the ladies-in-waiting, "Stay here. If I see you outside this room, you'll die, do you understand?" Of course I had no intention of harming them, but they both looked ready to faint. They wouldn't be a problem.

Throwing open the door, we stepped over the still unconscious guard. All the way down the hallway she twisted and tried to jerk her arm free from my grasp. I pushed her up against the wall and put my sword very near her throat.

"Listen to me! I haven't the time for this! Now you walk quickly, or I swear I will run you through!"

"It will be a pleasure watching you hang," she spat.

"If hanging means spending less time with you, then I happily choose the rope," I said. "Now move!"

I grabbed her by the back of the neck and held my sword at her back. We reached the staircase and stumbled our way down. I took a tighter grip on Eleanor and stepped through the door into the courtyard. By even laying a hand on Richard's mother, I had already committed a hanging offense. But I didn't care. I wasn't giving them Maryam without a fight.

"Sir Hugh!" I shouted.

He was standing less than thirty paces away. When he saw me, I could see his face in the torchlight, and his eyes went round with horror when he realized I held the Queen Mother. The Captain and a few of his guards started toward me.

"Stay where you are!" I shouted. "Another step and she dies!"

The guards skidded to a stop, all of them looking to the Captain for instruction.

"Release her, squire!" Sir Hugh shouted.

"Not until you free Maryam! Captain! Tell your men to cut her down!" I shouted.

"I don't make a move until you release the Queen Mother," the Captain replied.

"Have your men bring three horses, saddled and ready. Open the gate. Do it now!" I ignored him.

The Captain hesitated.

"Do what he says, Captain. There's no doubt he's quite mad!" the Queen Mother shouted. Finally she sounded a little afraid. Luckily, I had managed to convince her I was serious.

"You heard her!" the Captain ordered his men. The rumble of the gate echoed off the stone walls as it slowly rose. Then everything went quiet.

"Let her down, Sir Hugh!" I said.

"No!" he shouted back.

"Good. I'll look forward to hearing you explain to King Richard how you got his mother killed," I warned him.

"In case you've forgotten, boy, I'm a Templar. Do you think I care what a King thinks?" he sneered.

The Queen Mother tensed at this. Whatever scheme they had allied themselves in, it involved King Richard somehow. Or so I thought. These people were insane. Who knew what they were up to? But Eleanor let out a quiet hiss, as she clearly did not like her son being so easily dismissed by someone she considered nowhere near his equal.

Peering over the Queen Mother, I found Robard behind the wagon. He squatted there, his arrow nocked. He was coiled and ready, listening intently to every word and waiting for my signal.

The stable doors banged open, and guards led three mounts to the center of the courtyard. The Captain took a few steps closer to me.

"All right, squire, we've done everything you asked. Now let her go," he implored.

"Not yet. Order Sir Hugh to release Maryam. When my friends are on their horses, we'll discuss our next move."

The Captain faced Sir Hugh. "You heard him, sire—time to let her go. They won't get far. We'll catch them again soon enough."

Sir Hugh shook his head, the strain evident on his face as he pulled his sword. The Captain saw something in his eyes he didn't like and drew his own weapon.

"No, Captain. She stays where she is," Sir Hugh said, pointing his sword at the Captain's chest. "Not another step."

Sir Hugh looked wildly around the bailey. He was sweating and about to fall apart. In his own perverse way, he had come as far as I had in his quest. He had followed me like a bloodhound, only to be thwarted at every turn, just when the Grail was within his grasp. The look on his face now was one of a man who knew the chances of realizing his dream were growing dimmer by the second. If we escaped, if we left this castle, the Grail would elude him once more. He couldn't accept it.

"Sir Hugh!" the Captain pleaded. "You must stand down, sire. Don't make the situation worse. I trust my men. The prisoners won't get far."

But it was not to be. Sir Hugh said nothing, and even the Queen Mother tensed as the moments went by.

"Listen, boy," the Queen Mother whispered to me. "Let *me* go and I'll have my guards arrest Sir Hugh."

"No, your highness. Sir Hugh will kill her before your men can approach him. Be quiet."

"But you heard him. He's crazy now. Doesn't even care if I die, though Richard would hunt him down and kill him. What do you have that he wants so badly?" she hissed.

"Quiet, both of you!" Sir Hugh shouted at us, having heard our whispered conversation and grown unsettled by it. "Or she dies!"

"I have nothing. He's guilty of crimes against the Order—" I started my standard lie to the Queen Mother.

"Posh!" she interrupted me. "I don't believe you! Sir Hugh wouldn't be going to all this trouble for something as meaningless as crimes against the Order. What is it squire, gold? Give it to him. I'll give you more. Just let me go."

"You don't have enough gold, your majesty," I said, looking at Maryam standing precariously on the barrel.

Sir Hugh was still watching us intently, straining to hear what we said. He slowly twirled his sword in front of him. Behind him, two of the Captain's men crept stealthily forward.

"Captain! Tell your men to hold! If they touch him and Maryam dies, I will strike her down!" I warned him.

Sir Hugh whirled at my words, his sword at the ready, facing the men to his rear. Robard started to rise, but I shook my head, afraid if he shot now and Sir Hugh fell into the barrel, Maryam would still die. He grimaced in frustration but crouched behind the wagon again, waiting.

"Everyone stay calm!" the Captain shouted. He waved at his men and they retreated into the darkness. Sir Hugh turned back to us.

"All right, squire," he said. "I am weary of this. Give me what I want. I'll count to ten. If it's not in my hands, she dies." For emphasis, he moved behind Maryam and put his sword at her back. "Rope or blade, it makes no difference to me, squire." Maryam raised her head, her eyes slowly coming into focus. She looked around the courtyard, but I don't think she really knew where she was yet.

The Queen Mother still wouldn't remain silent. "What do you want, squire? Land? A title? You only need tell me and it's yours." Her voice had risen in pitch, and she chattered on nervously.

"What I want is for you to be silent," I whispered, "and my friend to be released."

"You must have something quite valuable for Hugh to be acting this way. What is it? I can help you, squire." She tried to wiggle from my grasp but I held fast. She was confusing me. I had expected her to fight, not negotiate. I had no interest in anything she said, but her constant prattle was distracting.

Robard peeked over the side of the wagon again and our eyes met. His face was a mask of rage, and he shook his head vigorously toward Sir Hugh as if imploring me to do something and soon. I nodded slightly, taking a deep breath.

"Do you have a death wish, my lady? If so, keep talking," I whispered to Eleanor. "Captain, on my honor as a Templar, I swear I will run her through and not think twice about it! Your choice! Richard will see you hang, Captain! Let her go, now!"

The Captain drew a breath and his shoulders slumped. He truly had no idea what to do and would undoubtedly have cut off a hand if it would have freed him from this place in time. Yet he knew where his duty lay. Slowly he turned to face Sir Hugh, but before he could do or say anything, Eleanor took action.

"Captain!" she shouted. "Listen to me clearly!"

Everyone stopped, even Sir Hugh, and stared at her.

"If I die, if anything happens to me, KILL THEM ALL! Sir Hugh included! Do you understand my orders?" The Captain clearly did not, for he cocked his head in confusion, and Sir Hugh's eyes went wide as he stared at her in amazement.

Then Eleanor of Aquitaine twisted her neck in my grasp, looking out at me from one evil eye. "If I die, so be it, boy," she said. "But I'll see you dead before you *ever* sit on Richard's throne."

A familiar feeling came over me. Time slowed, and I saw everything before me with the clarity of a circling hawk. It had happened before in Outremer on the battlefield and again when Robard had accidentally shot me. Every movement lags. Each sound becomes a muted symphony, and my senses are honed so sharply, I feel as if the air around me tastes of lightning. Another life-and-death moment was at hand.

This time there was a new feeling as befuddlement overwhelmed me. It was as if Eleanor's words had pulled me without warning from the deepest slumber. I lost my concentration for a brief moment. In a split second, may God forgive me, I paused to consider what she had said. She would see me dead before I sat on Richard's throne? What could she possibly mean?

And in my short moment of contemplation, whatever clue I gave away in my stance or eyes or the look on my face, in that brief instance Sir Hugh saw his chance.

He was still too far away for any of us to reach him, and knowing this he reared back with his right leg. I watched in terrified fascination as it started its inevitable descent forward toward the barrel. In less time than I could draw a breath Maryam was going to die.

Then as it had many times before, the stillness of time was

broken by a familiar humming sound that filled the air around me. Angel barked and everyone was screaming, but in my heightened state all sounds became faint and far away.

"Robard! Now!" I shouted. My own voice sounded dull, like I had tried to shout to him from under water. My body tensed, then sprang into action. With my eyes on Maryam, I pushed the Queen Mother roughly toward the Captain and sprinted for the wagon and Sir Hugh. There was a flicker of movement in the corner of my vision as Robard rose and took aim.

He let the arrow fly.

## To be continued . . .

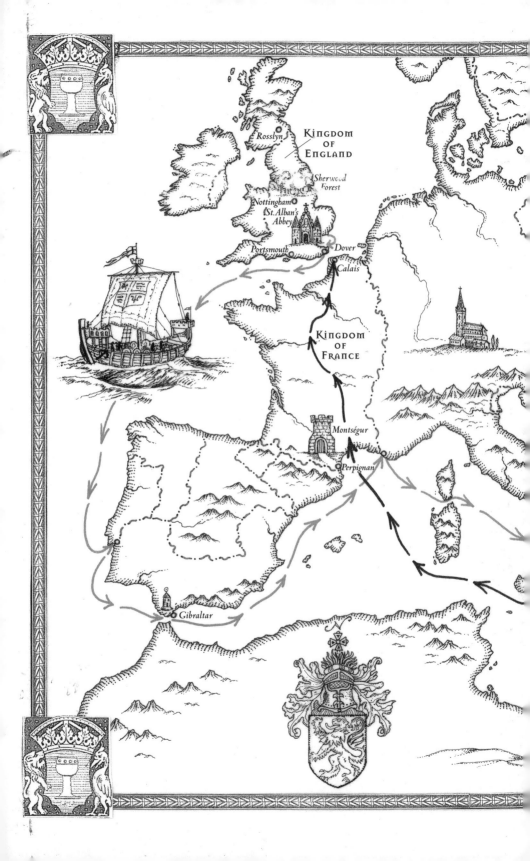

Rosslyn

KINGDOM
OF
ENGLAND

Sherwood
Forest

Nottingham
St. Alban's
Abbey

Portsmouth
Dover
Calais

KINGDOM
OF
FRANCE

Montségur

Perpignan

Gibraltar